A Bronx Tale 2

Lock Down Publications and Ca$h
Presents
A Bronx Tale 2
A Novel by *Ghost*

A Bronx Tale 2

Lock Down Publications
P.O. Box 870494
Mesquite, Tx 75187

Visit our website @
www.lockdownpublications.com

Copyright 2019 A Bronx Tale 2

Lock Down Publications
Like our page on Facebook: Lock Down Publications @
www.facebook.com/lockdownpublications.ldp
Cover design and layout by: **Dynasty Cover Me**
Book interior design by: **Shawn Walker**
Edited by: **Lauren Burton**

Stay Connected with Us!

Text **LOCKDOWN** to 22828 to stay up-to-date with new releases, sneak peaks, contests and more…

Thank you.

Submission Guideline.

Submit the first three chapters of your completed manuscript to ldpsubmissions@gmail.com, subject line: Your book's title. The manuscript must be in a .doc file and sent as an attachment. Document should be in Times New Roman, double spaced and in size 12 font. Also, provide your synopsis and full contact information. If sending multiple submissions, they must each be in a separate email.

Have a story but no way to send it electronically? You can still submit to LDP/Ca$h Presents. Send in the first three chapters, written or typed, of your completed manuscript to:

LDP: Submissions Dept
Po Box 870494
Mesquite, Tx 75187

DO NOT send original manuscript. Must be a duplicate.

Provide your synopsis and a cover letter containing your full contact information.

Thanks for considering LDP and Ca$h Presents.

Ghost

Chapter 1

Jahmani

I tried my best to put one foot in front of the other, though I couldn't help dragging my right foot along the concrete floor of the Bronx River House Projects. It smelled like urine and feces. The air was so thick I could taste it.

A thunderous storm was taking place outside of the eighteen-story building. Harsh winds coupled with rain and rocked the building's foundation, causing it to slightly sway. I held the graffiti-ridden walls for support while I attempted to keep up as best as I could with Samantha, my brother Pacho's daughter's mother.

Blood oozed from the gunshot wound in my thigh and ran directly into my right Jordan before spilling over it. With every step I took, the pain seemed to grow worse, but I had to fight to keep moving forward. I had to get to my mother and niece before Beans and his crew had the chance to.

I clenched my teeth together and sped up my limping, covering as much ground as I could. Lightning flashed across the sky outside. It was followed by a loud boom from the thunder. New York was feeling the after-effects of Hurricane Florence, which had hit the Carolinas with a vengeance. All the streets in the city were flooded, and most of the power had gone out.

I watched Samantha turn the corner that led up to my mother's apartment. She had to be about twenty feet ahead of me. Those twenty feet seemed more like a million because of the pain shooting from the hole in my thigh. I closed my eyes against the pain, then opened them seconds later, willing myself forward.

"Oh my God! Oh my God. Father, please, no! No!"

Samantha screamed from around the corner.

This sent chills down my spine. I turned my limping into a full-on jog, the pain no longer playing factoring in my brain. Lightning flashed across the sky outside of the projects. Thunder roared like an angry lion. I could hear the rain as it beat against the sidewalk outside. Its scent mixed with that of urine and feces, causing my stomach to turn. My heart beat rapidly in my chest. I felt like I couldn't breathe. I rushed and turned the corner in pursuit of Samantha.

My phone started to vibrate again. Minutes prior I'd received a call from Ari telling me somebody was outside of her home. Somebody? She never said who, but I could only imagine that somebody meant my cousin Linx.

A little more than a week ago I'd been forced to beat him senseless after he'd pointed a gun in my face and tried to kill Ari in front of me. After the beating, I made off with $500,000 of his money and a few kilos of heroin. Money, I knew he'd eventually come back for. Linx, like myself, was deadly. He killed with no remorse or regard for human life. I honestly didn't feel like he possessed a conscience, unlike myself. Every kill bothered me afterward. Every kill invaded my dreams and my thoughts at the wrong time. Every kill haunted me.

Five big, black rats ran across my path with their yellow teeth bared. They looked like raccoons. I could smell their stink. One stopped and hissed at me, stood up on its hind leg, and opened its mouth wide. I jumped back, a stinging pain shooting up through my right leg. I stomped at the pavement and aimed my gun at it, ready to shoot. Instead of the rat running away, it made its way toward me and stopped, stood on its feet, and sniffed the air while its friends ran along the wall away from me. I stomped my foot a second time. It hissed, then ran off, looking back at me twice before retreating around the corner. Sweat dripped down my back, making me itchy. I rushed forward, on the path to Samantha.

When I got to the beginning of the hallway where my mother's apartment was. I saw Samantha outside the door on her knees, rocking back and forth. She looked over at me with tears in her eyes. She got up and rushed into the house, whimpering, "Please, God, don't let this be."

I ran down the hall the rest of the way, stopped in front of my mother's apartment, and got sick. The first thing I noticed was the blood all over the door and wall. There seemed to be more of it leaking out into the hallway from the apartment.

When Samantha rushed inside, I guessed she'd accidentally bumped the door, causing it to come within a few inches of closing. I placed my hand on the door and slowly opened it, my heart thumping in my chest. My throat felt dry. I was both worried and afraid of what I was about to discover.

Not only was Samantha mixed up with some real grimy niggas, but me and Linx were at each other's heads. I knew from experience anything was on the table. Wasn't nobody exempt from our beef.

I pushed open the door all the way and saw the light to my mother's crib was out. I could hear Samantha somewhere in the back, whimpering. I didn't know what that meant. I stepped past the door jam, and onto the wet carpet. It squished under my Jordan. The apartment smelled like Febreeze and copper, or dried blood. I slid my hand along the wall, searching for the light switch that I knew was there. I found it and swiped my hand upward, clicking it, but nothing happened. I found that odd.

"Yo, Samantha, where you at, shorty? What the fuck going on?" I asked, easing further into the house. Now I had my gun held in front of me, ready to blow. I couldn't see nothing but slight images of things I was accustomed to being in my mother's crib. The carpet got wetter and wetter the further I got inside.

"Where is my baby, Jahmani? I'm about to lose my mind," she yelled, making her way back into the living room where I was.

"Yo, I can't see shit in here. The storm must've knocked the lights out. This carpet wet as hell, though. It smell like blood."

Samantha grabbed my arm. "Don't say that shit, Jahmani. Don't jinx them. It can't be blood. It just can't be," she cried, holding my arm tighter and tighter.

"Chill out, ma. You about to freak me the fuck out," I snapped, digging my hand into my pocket for my lighter. Once I found it, I pulled it out and held the flame up. I knew my mother had candles all around her place. I just needed to locate one so I could see what the hell was going on. I limped over to her living room table and picked up a long candle from it, lighting the tip just as my lighter got so hot. I dropped it to the carpet, then I stuck my thumb in my mouth to soothe the burning.

Samantha took the candle from me and ran it along the carpet, hunched over. She hadn't done this for more than ten seconds before she screamed at the top of her lungs. "Ah! Oh my God, Jahmani, look what they did to her!" she screamed. The candle dropped from her hand and fell to the carpet. It stayed lit for a second before going back out.

My eyes bugged out of my head. I searched along the carpet for my lighter and couldn't locate it. "Who is it, Samantha? Fuck, where is that lighter?" I snapped before saying fuck it and rushing beside her.

"It's Inez! I think she's dead!" she cried out loud.

I felt like I was about to faint. I felt all around in the dark with my arm outstretched until my hand came upon a face.

Lightning cut crazy zig-zags into the black sky, illuminating the apartment for a brief second.

"Momma! Momma! Ah!" I shrieked.

My mother was laid up against the wall with her head tilted backward and a gash in her throat. Her eyes were wide open and unseeing.

I picked her up into my arms and rushed out into the lit hallway, where I fell to my knees and lowered her to the concrete. "Momma! Aw, shit!" Tears ran out of my eyes and down my cheeks. My stomach turned upside down. "Why the fuck is she naked?"

There was the sound of thunder, then all the lights blinked off. Rain pelted against the ground outside. I could hear the whistle of the wind, then the sound of thunder growling. It got cold in the hallway. Off in the distance, six pair of red eyes stared down at me.

I dry-heaved and threw up after turning my back to my mother's dead body. Another lightning bolt illuminated the hallway, followed by thunder. The lights flashed back on, even the ones inside of my mother's apartment. I could hear Samantha inside, ransacking the place. "Where is Lonnie? Please, Father, don't let nothing be wrong with my baby," she cried from inside.

I crawled back to my mother and picked her up in my arms, looking down into her beautiful face. I closed her eyelids and rocked back and forth with her in my arms. "What happened, Momma? What happened to you?" I cried, on the verge of breaking down.

About twelve big, cat-sized rats closed in on us with their noses sniffing the air. Two of them stopped to lick up my mother's blood that puddled around us.

I closed my eyes and continued to rock with her. Defeated. Lost. Broken. Sick as if I had the flu. My mother was my heart and soul. The love of my life. The only one who had ever loved me unconditionally. I strived to become a better man for her. My goal was to move her out of the projects. Now she was gone, and I couldn't help but feel like I was responsible for her death in some way.

Samantha rushed out of the apartment and fell to her knees with blood all over her. "She's not in there, Jahmani, but I just got this text from Beans. Huh, read it." She thrust her phone in my face with tears dripping off her chin. She looked down at my mother and cried harder. "I'm so sorry, Inez."

I continued to hug my mother. "Just read the message, Samantha. Can't you see what they did to her?" I asked through a voice stricken with grief.

The rats closed in, and three of them crawled over my mother's bare foot. One of them dared to take a bite of her baby toe before I snapped, "Yah! Yah! Get the fuck out of here." I kicked at them. They scurried down the hallway, never looking back. I grabbed her closer to me and held her.

"'Bitch, bring me my money and my work, or you'll find your little girl in pieces. Signed, the Mobb,'" Samantha read the text from her phone. "I gotta get this money over to Beans, Jahmani, or they gon' kill Lonnie. Can you please come with me? I'm begging you," she cried, wrapping her right arm around my neck.

I don't know what it was, but something in me snapped. Now that I knew she was the cause for my mother being killed and it wasn't the many beefs I had, I snapped. I grabbed her by the throat and smacked her across the face so hard it caused her lip to split. She flew backward into the wall. I jumped up. "You punk-ass bitch! I told you not to go fucking with them Dyse Avenue niggas. Now look at what they did to my mother!" I grabbed her up by the hair so I could slap her again. This time she flew into my mother's doorframe and hit her face

12

on it, fell backward, and landing on her ass. Blood leaked from her lips. She scooted backward on her backside, looking up at me with wide eyes.

"What are you doing, Jahmani? It's not my fault. I said I was sorry. I swear it ain't my fault." She got to her feet, wiped her mouth, and spit blood onto the concrete.

I felt possessed. I made my way back toward her with murder on my mind. Somebody had to pay for my mother's death. Because Samantha had ripped the Crips off, they'd murdered my mother in cold blood. Murdered her and taken my niece. Now they were threatening to kill her as well, and it was all because of Samantha. All her fault. I was about to kill this bitch. I'd figure out my next move later.

"I'm sick of yo' shit, bitch! Every time you make a mistake, all you do is holler that sorry shit. I'm tired of that!" I balled my fists.

She backed away. Her eyes scanned the entire hallway until they came upon a two-by-four lying in front of the elevator. The board had originally been nailed to block the entrance of the elevator due to it being out of order, but somewhere along the way it had fallen off. She picked it up. "Stay away from me, Jahmani. Stay away, or I swear to God I'ma bust your shit with this board. Word is bond, I will. Now, I said I'm sorry."

Every time I heard her say she was sorry, it was like nails on a chalkboard. It made me want to kill her even more, so I continued to make my way toward her. I didn't think she had enough guts to hit me with a board. And besides, I didn't give a fuck. This bitch was responsible for the death of my mother. She had to pay.

We made it all the way to the end of the hallway. She pressed her back against the wall and tightened her grip on the block of wood. "I'm not playing, Jahmani. Stay away from me.

Stay away from me, please!"

I lowered my head and rushed her. I had visions of getting my hands around her throat again, but this time squeezing until the life sailed out of her body. I wanted this punk bitch dead. I wanted her to meet my mother in the afterlife, that way my mother could kick her ass.

I got within five feet of her when she cocked the wood all the way back before swinging it as hard as she could. At the same time, my right leg buckled, and I lost my balance. The two-by-four slammed into the left side of my neck, rocking me so hard I flew to my right and into the wall. Pain shot through me ASAP. It was so bad that I felt like screaming like a little kid.

"I'm tired of you putting your fucking hands on me, Jahmani! I said I was sorry!" She lifted the wood over her head and brought it down across my back, knocking me to the floor. My chin scraped against the concrete of the filthy hallway.

I groaned in pain and struggled to get up. "I'm finna kill you, bitch," I promised, in so much agony my vision was going blurry. I couldn't believe she was fucking me up like this.

She jumped in the air and brought the wood across my back again. *Bam!* "That is for the last time you kicked my ass!" *Bam!* Another whack across my back. This time it hurt so bad I blanked out for a few seconds. When I came to, she was kicking me in the ribs and flipping me on my back. I closed my eyes and struggled to take in enough air to breathe. My lungs felt like they were on fire. I opened my eyes and saw four of her. The world seemed to be spinning. Lightning flashed behind her. I felt around on my waist, searching for my pistol. I pulled it out and –

Bam! This time I felt the wood whack me across the jaw. My pistol flew out of my hand and down the hallway. I flipped over on my back, my head spinning like a top.

I rose up on my elbows and saw Samantha pick my gun up and rush back over to me. She aimed it into my face wit' tears streaming down hers. "I know you gon' kill me, Jahmani. You're crazy, just like your brother. I should take your life right now. Shouldn't I?" She wiped her face with her right hand and held the gun with her left. "Tell me not to kill you, Jahmani!"

My head was ringing. I could feel blood running down my neck. I felt weak and sick at the same time. The death of my mother was taking its toll on me as well. I looked up and saw five versions of Samantha. She looked as if she was in a fun house mirror. I didn't know which one was the real her, so spit at all of them. "Fuck you, bitch. I swear to God, you better kill me. Kill me right now. If you don't, whenever I get up, I got yo' ass. That's my word," I spat. No way could I let this go. This bitch had fucked me up after getting my mother killed. I wanted her blood on my hands. I couldn't see it no other way.

She stood looking down at me for a long time, then cocked the hammer of my pistol. "That's what I thought." She wiped her tears away. "I'm sorry, Jahmani. Please know I never meant for any of this to happen, but I can't let you get up off this floor." She lowered the gun and put her finger around the trigger.

She bit into her lower lip and squeezed the trigger just as I kicked her knee as hard as I could. *Boom. Boom.* The bullets slammed into the concrete beside my head.

She fell backward and hopped up and down on one leg before turning and running a short distance. She stopped and fired two more shots. *Boom. Boom.* "I'm sorry, Jahmani! Please know that!"

Boom. Boom. More shots in my direction. I rolled around on the floor and got to my feet, running as best I could down the hall until I tripped over my mother's body, falling to my knees in her blood. There were no more shots fired by Samantha, but the damage had been done. I wrapped my arms around my ribs and struggled to breathe.

I pulled my mother into my embrace and held her while the lights flickered on and off in the project building.

Chapter 2

I pulled my car around to the back alley of Ari's Brownstone. The wind had picked up by at least ten miles an hour. The rain was coming down so hard it felt like hail was beating across my back. The alley was flooded. Green garbage cans full of trash floated past me like small boats. It was dark and freezing. I felt sick to my stomach, woozy from the blood loss.

I opened the driver's door and activated the interior lights. My mother's body lay along the back seat, lifeless. In the trunk was Mardi's deceased father. He was the one who had shot me in the thigh while he made a play on my life.

When I jumped out of the car, I stepped into water that came up to my thighs. It smelled like pure sewage.

I struggled to make it up the stairs to Ari's back door, but by the grace of God I was successful. I fell against her door and beat on it. "Ari! Ari! Open the door, ma. It's me," I gasped, out of breath and with my eyes closed. I waited for a short time, then heard heavy footsteps.

"Jahmani! Is that you?" she hollered from the other side of the door.

I slid down to my ass. Everything finally starting to take a toll on me physically. "Yeah, ma. Open the door. I'm fucked up right now." My throat was dry, my stomach in knots. I just wanted to sleep. I wanted the pain to stop. I needed this to be a dream, one I would wake up from real soon.

"Jahmani, I can't see you in the peep hole. Please go in front of it. I ain't opening the door until I confirm it's you. Hurry up," she ordered. She sounded hysterical.

I used the wall to help me get to my feet. There was barely any strength left in my right leg. I pulled myself upward and fell with my left shoulder against her door. "It's me. Open up."

She pulled open the door, and I fell face-first, landing in a push-up position. "Oh my God, what happened to you, Jahmani?" She knelt and pulled me inside, then quickly stood up and locked the door, placing a two-by-four in front of it.

At the sight of the block of wood, my face began to throb, remembering the beating Samantha had given me. I crossed and placed my back up against her wall. "My mother's dead. They took my niece. I don't know where she is. I gotta get her back, though. Her mother fucked me up." I groaned in pain and got to my knees.

Ari placed her hand on my back. "Who killed your mother, Jahmani? Was it Linx? He was here. He shot into my bedroom window and said he'd be back. I called the police, and they still ain't been here yet. I'm so scared. He's crazy."

She helped me get to my feet and sat me in a chair that was up against the dining room table. I could feel myself leaking. "Samantha screwed over some Crip niggas. Took they money and shit. They killed my mother and took my niece. When I tried to get in her ass about it, she fucked me up wit' a two-by-four. I need you to stitch me up and get me right. I gotta find my niece." I winced in pain as a bolt of agony shot through me. It was so bad I slid out of the chair and fell to my knees, then my back. I lay straight out and closed my eyes. I needed the pain to go away.

She fell beside me and ran her hands over a bunch of my wounds. "Okay, I got you. Just stay right here." She rushed out of the room and toward the back of the house. Everything became blurry, so I closed my eyes, and took a deep breath. A lone tear seeped out of my left eyelid and slid down the side of   my cheek. It wound up in my ear canal. Visions of my mother's beautiful face entered my mind. I could mentally feel her in my arms the last time I'd been able to hug her. Her laugh. Her smile. Every sacrifice she'd made for me as a kid. All of it played over in my mind's eye. The pain in my heart was indescribable.

Ari rushed back into the room and knelt beside me. "Take these pants off. I can tell you're wounded on this leg." She pulled my pants down, freeing the injured thigh. As soon as the air hit it, I hollered out in pain and turned slightly on my side. "I'm sorry, Jahmani, but I gotta get to it," she advised, placing a black garbage bag underneath it. "How did this happen, anyway?" She removed her first aid items and started to get to work, first sterilizing the wound with rubbing alcohol.

I grabbed a handful of the carpet and clenched my teeth together. It felt like she was pouring acid into my thigh. "Ah! Fuck, Ari!" I was breathing hard with my eyes closed tightly.

"That's why you gotta keep talking, so you don't worry about what I'm doing down here. Now, tell me what happened, and let me handle my business. I got you."

Sweat slid from my forehead. I could hear the thunderstorm still going full blast outside of her window. Lightning flashed and the lights of her apartment threatened to go out. I looked into her pretty brown eyes and nodded my head. "Awright. Mardi's punk-ass father did this. His name is Mason. Ah! Shit!" I curled my toes on my right foot in a mock attempt to diffuse some of the pain I was feeling all over, but it was of no use.

"Just keep talking, Jahmani. Why would he do this to you?" She continued to dab at the wound with an alcohol-drenched pad before pinching my skin together and taking out her sewing kit, preparing to stitch me up.

"Mardi took over $500,000 in cash from me while I was over here with you. She was the only person I had ever shown where my stash was at. I wish I never had, 'cause she fucked me worse than ever. I knew she messed with her old man real tough, so I went over there looking for her, and he got out of pocket. Got to talking all crazy and whatnot. Long story short, me and the old head got into a confrontation. He wound up shooting me, and let's just say things didn't fare too well for him after that."

My eyes rolled into the back of my head as she sewed me up with an expert-like technique. She looked focused and determined to get me right. "Yo, so is that the reason you ran out of here so fast without letting me know what the deal was?" She looked into my eyes, pausing briefly in her stitching.

"Yeah. No offense, ma, but we just getting to know each other. It's been a lot of stuff going on that I ain't put you in tune with. I think it's for your own safety, though. My world is bananas right now. It's crazy. But I ain't gotta tell you that, seeing as this is the second time you've had to fix me up in less than a month." I laid all the way back and covered my eyes with my left arm.

"Well, my life ain't all peachy, either. I lost my brother, I just lost my cousin, and now I got this lunatic stud Linx on my heels. It's only a matter of time before I'm somewhere being stitched up. I just pray he doesn't take my life. I don't know if I'm ready to go just yet." She sighed and went right back to getting me together.

"Yo, ain't nothing about to happen to you, goddess. On my word, I'd die before I let that nigga hurt you. Fuck that," I snapped, sitting partway up with sweat dripping down my face. I was in excruciating pain.

"I appreciate you saying that, Jahmani. You sound pretty genuine. I honestly hope he just goes away. I've never done anything to him. I don't know why he can't get that through his head. He thinks I set him up to be robbed by Mikey when all along I had no idea Mikey was even thinking about doing something to him. I would have warned him, or at the very least tried to talk Mikey out of it. Everybody knows Linx is nuts." She went back to sewing me up.

20

I'd only known Ari for a matter of months, but it was something about this female that had me captivated. She was about five feet, six inches tall and dark caramel-colored with a beautiful face with light freckles strategically placed all over it. If I had to guess, I'd say she weighed in somewhere between one thirty and one forty. Her body was immaculate. On top of that, she had these real deep dimples that appeared on each cheek every time she spoke. Dimples that left me in a trance. Even though she was one of the most mature women I'd ever met, she gave off this childlike energy. She was tough, yet vulnerable. I knew she could hold her own, but at the same time a part of me needed to protect her. I needed to be her shield, even if she didn't want me to be. I had to be honest with myself. I cared about her already, even though I was holding two secrets that I knew whenever she found out about them, she would hate my guts with a passion and probably never want anything to do with me for as long as she lived.

The first secret: I'd been the one who killed her only brother. He'd tried to rob my brother's baby mother, Samantha, and myself for a large sum of money, but I couldn't let that shit happen. In the end he wound up losing his life.

If that wasn't bad enough, the second secret also involved murder, but this time I'd not been the one behind the trigger. I'd taken part in the robbery and murder of her cousin, Mach. He'd been the last surviving male in her family who she was close to.

Those two secrets were eating me up inside, and I knew I had to get them out of me. I just didn't know when they would surface or how I'd give them to her. The man in me would not allow me to hold them in for long. I felt like she deserved to know the truth, and one day I would give it to her.

She finished sewing up my thigh and started to work on other minor area. "Jahmani, I thought you and Mardi were close, but now you're saying she stole all of that money from you? Damn, that's foul. She doesn't even look like the type who would get down like that. She always spoke about how much she loved you and all of the things you've done for her." She shook her head. "I just don't get it. When you say her father didn't fare well, what do you mean?"

"Yo, ma, the less you know, the better. I ain't trying to involve you in none of this. Just handle yo' bidness and get me right. I gotta figure some shit out in my head. Straight up." I balled my hands into fists and started to miss my mother again. Then Lonnie crossed my mind. I needed to get her back. I didn't trust Samantha to get the job done. I knew how them Dyse Avenue Crips got down. They were deadly. They'd been a thorn in the side of the residents of the Bronx River House Projects for almost five years now. Them cats ain't have no love or regard for humanity. I was scared my niece Lonnie was already dead. If that was the case, I would have to go at them niggas with everything I had.

Ari shook her head and kept on working. "I just don't understand how we're going to figure things out if you won't even tell me what's really good. Then another thing, you're way too intelligent to always have curse words flying off your tongue. That is so unattractive." She frowned and remained focus on her task of repairing my injuries.

I rose up on my elbow and mugged her. "Shorty, it's so much going on in my life right now that the only way I can express myself is through cursing. I feel like killing up a neighborhood of muthafuckas right now. My mother was my life, goddess. Yo, I'm losing my fucking mind right now over her loss. Then them same chumps got my niece somewhere hemmed up. Yo, cursing is all I got, so excuse me if I've offended you in any way."

She shrugged her shoulders. "It's good. I mean, I guess I

understand where you're coming from. Nobody should have to endure what you are. It's not fair, but if anybody can sympathize with you, it's me. So just know I'm here for you. Whatever it takes, just let me know, and I'll do my best. I mean that."

As angry as I was at hearing those words, for some reason they brought me comfort. I calmed down just a bit, lay back on the floor, and closed my eyes. "Ma, just get me right. Get me right and I'll make sure you're good. That's my word."

"Oh, I am, but you don't owe me anything. You saved my life. You stopped Linx from killing me, and for that reason I am forever in your debt." She crawled across the carpet and kissed me on the cheek, then rubbed it away with her thumb before retreating and finishing the job.

***

It took her a total of five hours to stitch everything that needed stitching. After she finished, she gave me a washcloth and drying towel and instructed me to handle my hygiene. She took my dirty clothes and washed them for me. By the time I came out of the bathroom, everything was clean. I felt a little better, though I was still in agony.

I stepped out of the bathroom to find her in the living room, on her knees wit' her hands clasped together in prayer. I stood at a distance, watching in silence until she finished five minutes later, looked back at me, and smiled.

"I could feel you standing there the whole time. It took every ounce of concentration I had to not turn around and tell you to join me." She stood up and walked over to me, touching each of the bandages. "How do you feel?"

I nodded my head, then shook it. "I'm in pain. I can't take it. It's killing me right now. You ain't got nothing here you can inject me with to take the edge off from this misery?" I asked, holding my jaw. I could still feel the impact from the two-by-four Samantha had used on me. I was gon' kill that bitch when I caught her. I knew that for a fact.

Ari ran her hand over my face and rubbed my jaw ever so lightly. "Nall, I ain't got nothing I can inject into you. They don't put them in first aid kits."

She looked into my eyes and rested her hand on my naked chest. Her finger grazed over the long scar her brother had given me when he'd stabbed me with a steak knife in the chest. Her touch seemed to be healing me, yet at the same time it brought a bout of guilt.

"What happened to you here? I don't think you've ever told me."

I stared at her fingers that traced over the scar tissue for a long time. "Aw, you know how it is in the Bronx. Some nigga tried to rob me with a knife. He jammed it in there pretty good. It is what it is. I'm still here." I took her hand away and kissed the back of it, holding my lips on it maybe longer than I should have. "Ari, thank you for sewing me up. Yo, if I'da went to one of these hospitals, they'da had a million questions. They probably would have put me in a cell and everything. Whatever you need from me, let me know right now, and I got you." I kissed her hand again and rubbed it along the side of my face. She smelled so good.

She pulled her hand back and blushed, turning her back to me. "It's good. I already told you I'm in your debt. I wouldn't even be here if it wasn't for your protection." She hugged her body and exhaled loud enough for me to hear her.

I couldn't deny taking the time to glance at the swell of her backside as it poked out of her tight-fitting skirt. Man, she was so strapped. Built like a goddess from Africa.

I placed my hand on her shoulder, then slowly turned her

around to face me. I looked into her brown eyes and smiled. "I don't know what I'm about to do, but I gotta avenge my mother's death and get my niece back before it's too late. I know we just getting to know each other and all, but I need to know you gon' be here when I get back." I placed my hand on the side of her soft cheek and brushed my thumb back and forth across it, looking into her eyes. Damn, she was so fine.

She wiggled out of my embrace and turned her back on me again. "Jahmani, ain't nothing in those streets but death. You've come to me two times in need of repair. I'm afraid the third time I won't be able to repair you. I'm scared for your sake and mine." She walked over to the table, placed her left hand on it, and lowered her head. "I swear, I don't know what to do."

I came and stood on the side of her, rubbing her back. "I need to protect you, Ari. I need to make sure nothing happens to you. I need to get you up out of the Bronx."

"Jahmani, both of us need to get out of here. With that fool Linx on the loose, along with those guys that hurt your mother, there is no telling how long we have before one or the both of us is lying somewhere dead. Now, we have to be smart. We have our whole lives ahead of us."

I shook my head and walked away from her, picked up my freshly-washed Jordans, and slid them onto my feet. They were still a bit damp on the inside, but not enough that it was uncomfortable. The shoes looked wrinkled from the wash. I knew as soon as I got the chance, I would throw them away and replace them.

"Yo, I see what you getting at, and even though it makes sense, I can't let this shit with my mother go unanswered. And I can't leave my niece out in the cold. If you're asking me to do that, then maybe it's best we part ways. I'll catch you on the rebound or something." I left the living room and went into her bedroom, grabbing my guns and the five hundred dollars in cash I had left to my name. I put the pistols on my hip and made my way toward the front of the house. I found her standing at the table with her head down. I could tell she was defeated.

I spun her around to face me and pulled her into my embrace. I didn't care if she wanted me to hug her or not. At this point, she really didn't have a choice. I held her firmly and kissed her perfumed neck. "I appreciate everything you've done for me. I pray I see you again. I know if all this stuff wouldn't have ever happened, you and I would have shared a strong bond, and maybe even more. I swear you're the finest female I've ever laid eyes on. I will never forget you." I kissed her neck and inhaled her womanly scent, taking it into my memory bank.

She slowly wrapped her arms around my neck and hugged me back. "Jahmani, it doesn't have to end like this. I'm just getting to know you, and I like the man I see. All I'm saying is we should approach this ordeal from another angle because sometimes fighting fire with fire will only cause an explosion." She hugged me tighter and grazed my ear with her soft lips.

The feel of her in my embrace felt magical. It felt right. She felt perfect. Soft, feminine, and vulnerable. I didn't want to let her go, but I knew I had to because if I didn't, then I would never avenge my mother or be able to rescue my niece, and both of those things I had to do. There was no way around them in my heart.

I hugged her for a short while longer, then released her. I held her wrists. "I swear I don't wanna leave you, Ari, but I gotta handle my bidness. Here." I took one of the Glock .40s from my waist and tried to hand it to her.

She took a step back and held her hands up at shoulder

height. "What are you giving me that for? I don't know how to use it."

I stepped toward her and popped it off safety. "It's easy, ma. Look, I'll give you a quick lesson right now. C'mere."

She shook her head. "No, I can't. I'm scared of guns. They've done nothing but hurt the people I love. It's only a matter of time before they hurt me." She bit the fingernail of her right index finger.

I shook my head. "Nall, ma, we ain't gon' let that happen. Let me show you what's good."

I held the gun out and watched her back up into the wall in fear. It tripped me out. Her eyes got bucked. She looked past me and toward the front door. "Oh my God." Both of her hands went to the sides of her face. She looked as if she was about to panic.

I frowned. "What's the matter wit' you?" I looked her over closely, the gun still in my right hand. Then I heard the heavy footsteps. It sounded like a bunch of them coming up the stairs of her Brownstone.

She rushed past me, and to the big window of her living room. "Oh my God. We gotta get out of here, right now!"

Ghost

Chapter 3

"Wait, what are you looking at?" I ran over to the window and looked out of it. In front of her building were five black Eddie Bauer trucks with their doors wide open. The streets were flooded, and the rain was coming down harder than before. There was a pounding on her front door that scared the shit out of me. I jumped and felt goosebumps rise all over my arms.

Ari rushed toward the back of her apartment and into her bedroom. I watched her pull a pair of pants up her legs, then she threw on a pair of Airmax. Her eyes were as big as I had ever seen them. She waved at me to come to her.

The pounding on the door turned to kicks. *Whoom!* *Whoom!* *Whoom!* "Bitch, open this muthafucking door before I kick this bitch in. I told you I was coming back," Linx hollered.

I knew that voice from anywhere, and I could tell he meant business. I ran in front of the door and pointed my gun at it, ready to blow a bunch of holes through it right where I knew his head would be. I figured if I could knock his brains out of his melon, then the war with him would be over and done with. I cocked both Glocks and got ready to bust.

Just as he started to kick the door again, Ari ran over and grabbed me by the right arm. "Jahmani, come on. We can go down the fire escape before he knocks it down. Let's go!" she said in a panic.

I pushed her away. "Nall, fuck that. I'm finna kill this nigga right here and right now. Word is bond." I lowered my eyes and bit my bottom lip.

She grabbed my shirt and pulled me in her direction. "Please, Jahmani. I'm riding with you. Let's just get out of here."

I looked into her eyes and saw them tearing up. I hated the

sight of that. I nodded my head. "Awright, you go ahead, and I'ma be right behind you. I'ma buy us a little time. Now go." I pushed her toward the back door.

She grabbed a big Prada jacket with a hood, then opened the door wide before disappearing out of it.

The kicks started on the door again. I counted to sixty in my head, then backed up just a little before I got to dumping at the door. *Boom. Boom. Boom. Boom. Boom.* Big holes knocked chunks out of the wood. I heard somebody holler out in pain, and then I was jetting out of the back door, running behind Ari with my thigh killing me.

The rain attacked my face, along with the harsh winds as I rushed down the escape stairs, holding onto the railing for leverage. I could look down and see Ari going as fast as she could. Twice she slipped and jumped back up. I was happy to see her do so. The alley looked like a rushing river, it was so flooded. Sparks of electricity flashed across the sky, lighting it up for a full second, and then it was pitch black again. I could feel my heart beating faster and faster as I traveled down the stairs.

"They out here. I see them. It's two of them. She's with some nigga!" a voice yelled.

And then the shooting started. *Boom. Boom. Boom.* Sparks flew off the metal stairs. Bullets whizzed by my head. This caused me to panic. I stumbled and lost my balance, slipping and falling down three hard stairs, and landing on my knees. I took my pistol and aimed it upward. *Boom. Boom. Boom. Boom. Click. Click. Click.* I jumped up and continued on my way. More shots were fired in our direction. Their bullets whizzed past my head and struck the metal.

Down below, I watched Ari jump off the last stair and take off running down the alley as best she could. The water came up a few inches above her knees.

Boom. Boom. Boom. "That's that bitch-nigga Jahmani. Kill him, Blood. He got our scratch!" Linx yelled. *Bocka. Bocka. Bocka. Bocka. Bocka. Bocka.* His bullets came in rapid fashion.

Up ahead, Ari fell face-first into the water and didn't get up. My eyes bugged out of my head. I started to lose my mind. "Ari! Ari! Aw, shit!" My knees touched my chest as I ran as fast as I could in the filthy water, trying not to pay attention to how much of it went inside of my mouth. I had to get to her. I had to save her. I had to keep her alive, so I ran as fast as I could until I was standing over the spot where she'd fallen.

Once there, I felt around until I bumped into her body. I took ahold of her jacket and pulled her up as more and more bullets were fired in our direction. "Ari! Ari! Are you okay?" I hollered, wiping the water out of her pretty face.

She held her shoulder. "I'm shot, Jahmani. Oh my God, I'm shot! It hurts so bad," she screamed and fell against me.

"Fuck, man!" I felt like I'd been gut-punched. I wrapped her left arm around my neck and continued to rush down the alley as best as I could, holding her up. "Come on, baby. Fight. We gon' make it. I promise we gon' make it. I got you," I assured. She leaned against me. I could hear her whimpering. I knew she had to be in some serious pain. I'd been shot in the shoulder before, and it felt like the worst kind of pain you could possibly imagine. I wished I could have taken the bullet for her.

Boom. Boom. Boom. Boom. Boom. Boom. I looked over my shoulder and saw Linx dressed in an all-black hoodie. He held a chrome .45 in his hand, finger-fucking the trigger again and again. "I'ma kill you, son! That's my word!" He started to run with his knees rising high out of the water.

I held Ari tighter and sped up the pace. Water dripped down the back of my neck and into my collar. It felt like something was crawlin' on me. Little gnats were all over the surface of the water. The alley smelled like garbage and spoiled milk. I saw more than one dead cat floating along the river-like flood.

The rain picked up its intensity. I lifted Ari by the waist and ran uphill alongside a garage to steady myself. Once there, I allowed her to rest up against a gate. I kissed her on the cheek. "Baby, chill right here. Let me get at these niggas real quick. You hear me?"

She nodded her head as blood oozed through her fingers. "Okay, but please come back. I need you, Jahmani. I hate saying it, but it's the truth." She lowered her head and slid down the fence into a huge puddle of muddy water that smelled like death.

I wiped the rain away from my face as best I could and lowered my eyes, hatred for Linx entering my heart. I had to protect Ari. His bitch-ass had already put a slug in her. A slug that should have went inside of me. I was furious.

I kissed her on the forehead and jogged through the muddy water as best I could. I ignored the stabbing pain in my right thigh where Mardi's father had shot me. I couldn't allow it to dictate my actions. I ran to the neighbor's fence and hopped over it. I landed in a pool of filth. I jumped up and rushed alongside the neighboring garage until it led me back to the alley. Once there, I looked down it and saw Linx and one of his homies were still making their way in our direction. I waited and took a deep breath. I needed them to get a little closer. About twenty more feet.

I glanced over at Ari and saw her struggling to stand up. Her face was turned into a ball of pain. It gave me a heavy heart. It was my job to protect her, my job to make sure no harm ever came to her, but I had failed at that task. Failed miserably, and that pissed me off. I wanted to go over to console her, but the killer in me had to handle bidness first, so I waited like a patient hunter.

I peeked around the garage and saw they had gotten considerably closer. Linx's guy was no more than fifteen feet away from me. I knew I should wait until he got closer, but I couldn't. I had to murder both right now.

I ducked down and turned the corner of the garage, raised my Glock, and got to busting with no mercy. The first bullets smacked into Linx's homie's face and splattered it. He did a one-eighty before falling into the water with a loud splash.

Linx stopped dead in his tracks and raised a Tech .9. Where he'd gotten it from, I didn't know, but its clip was as long as a table leg. On top of it was a green beam. He aimed it at me and pulled the trigger. *Tat-tat-tat-tat-tat-tat-tat-tat.*

The bullets ate up the side of the garage. I ducked down and fell on my ass, airing at him. *Boom. Boom. Boom. Boom.* "Bitch-ass nigga!" *Boom. Boom. Boom. Boom. Boom.*

Linx fell into the water wit' his finger on the trigger of his weapon. *Tat-tat-tat-tat-tat-tat!* He jumped up and took off runnin' in the opposite direction, falling over and over.

I aimed and pulled the trigger of my Glock, finding it empty. I was thankful he'd retreated before I was exposed.

I turned and rushed back to Ari. She held herself up by using the fence. Her eyes were slits. Her entire jacket was filled with blood. When she saw me, she reached out to me and fell into my arms, weak.

"Ari, baby, stand up. Come on. We gotta get you to a hospital!" I hollered, picking her up on my shoulder and running through the murky waters with her. My chest hurt. I felt like I couldn't breathe. Both of my legs were cramping, along with stomach. My vision was hazy. I could feel blood running out of my stitches. There were so many bugs crawling all over me that I felt like I was about to lose my mind. But I had to save her. I had to get her to a hospital. I knew she was in the worst form of pain. I was gon' get that nigga Linx if it was the last thing I did.

When we came to the next block, it was just as flooded as the one her apartment was on. A light pole had fallen in the middle of the block. Electric sparks popped up from it into the air. The wind was so intense I felt like I was going to fall with her. I knew if I did, we'd be losing valuable time that could cost her life, so I couldn't let that happen. I had to save her.

I ran down the block with her in a frenzy. My legs felt like jelly. "Ari! Ari! Baby, you gotta keep talking to me. Keep them eyes open. Please, baby! Do you hear me?" I yelled.

"Yes. Yes. Jahmani. I hear you. It's so hard," she whispered.

I came alongside a black-on-black, 1996 Buick Century. I laid her on the hood and made sure she wouldn't slip. Once she was in place, I rushed to the side of the car, turned my gun around, and slammed it five times into the upper corner of the back window until it shattered. The alarm started to blare like crazy. *Er! Er! Er! Er! Er!* I knocked the glass out of the way and stuck my arm inside, unlocking the door and pulling it open. Once it was open, I rushed inside and into the front seat, where I found the wires under the steering wheel. I yanked them down and went through the process of hotwiring it. It took me less than two minutes before the engine roared to life. As soon as it did, I sat in the driver's seat and took ahold of the steering wheel, pulling it as hard as I could to one side, and then the opposite side with the same amount of brute force. The spring popped out of it and onto the floor mat. The steering wheel loosened up, letting me know I would be able to control it without a hassle.

I rushed out of the car toward Ari when the door opened to the brownstone the car was parked in front of. A big, heavyset man with a baseball bat in his hands came out of it with an angry look on his face. He ran toward the stairs and began to come down them, splashing water along the way. "You son of a bitch! Get away from my car. Get away from my car right now!" he ordered, jumping off the last three stairs.

Ari slid off the hood of the car and into the water, her head going under. She'd passed out from the blood loss. "Aw, shit." I rushed to her side and pulled her up. "Say, man, my girl been shot. I need to get her to a hospital. Help me, please," I pleaded, looking at the big, approaching monster.

He raised his hands to his forehead along with the bat. "Aw, muthafucka, you done broke my back window! I ain't even got insurance on this sucka. I'ma bust yo' head!" he snapped and rushed me with the bat held high over his head.

I ran at him before he could get to me. Ari slipped back into the flow of water, her face going under. As soon as I got close enough to him, he swung the bat and connected with my raised forearm. It made a loud clunking sound that made my left side go numb, but my velocity allowed me to tackle him against the stairs of his stoop. His head bouncing off them. I head-butted him in the face and kneed him in the nuts at the same time. "Punk-ass nigga. You gon' hit me wit' a bat?"

He hollered in pain, dropped the bat, and wrapped both of his big hands around my neck, lifting me in the air, choking me like crazy. My legs kicked wildly. I fought in his choke-hold. I couldn't breathe. I felt my air being blocked off. My eyes were watering horribly.

"I hate you li'l niggas! Hate you! Die, fuck-boy! Die!" he growled.

I smacked and clawed at his hands. It felt like ice was coming into my lungs. I passed gas back-to-back. This big gorilla was choking the life out of me.

He cocked me back and threw me onto his stoop stairs like

a rag doll. I crashed into the concrete railing and bounced off it, rolling into the water, gasping for breath.

"This my hood, li'l daddy. Word is bond. You gon' wish you never crossed the kid." He stomped his way over to me with wild eyes.

I forced myself up and held up my guards. As soon as he got close enough, I ran past his bitch-ass and picked up the baseball bat, cocked it all the way back, and swung, connecting with his chin. He doubled over. His big hand reaching for the concrete railing. He winced and hollered out in pain.

"Yeah, bitch-ass nigga! Choke me now, son! Choke me now!" *Bam*! I swung the bat as hard as I could, bringing it across his back after jumping in the air with it to bring down as much force as I possibly could.

He arched his back and fell to his face, then rolled onto his side, got up, and took off running down the block. Water splashed all around him as he made his escape. "I'ma catch you, money! Word is bond, I'ma catch you!" he hollered over his shoulder.

The pain in my throat made me want to chase after him, but from the corner of my eye I saw Ari's body twitching, and it snapping me out of my zone. I dropped the bat and rushed to her side. "Ari!" When I got there, I knelt and pulled her out of the water. She'd been face down for God only knows how long. Her eyes were closed. She looked as if she was turning blue. I placed my ear to her mouth and listened for some sort of air or anything that would tell me she was still alive, but I heard nothing.

I freaked out. "Oh my God!" I picked her up and laid her in the back seat of the Buick, giving her CPR before I blew into her mouth. "Come on, Ari. Come on, baby, please!" More compressions. Her eyes remained closed tightly. Her body jerked as my chest compressions continued. I placed my mouth over hers and breathed into it, pinching her nose. I prayed in my mind to the Lord above, begging Him to save her, to keep her alive. I couldn't lose her right now. I couldn't stand the loss. I didn't know what it would do to me, especially since I felt so responsible. First her shoulder, and now this. So, I blew and blew, praying for a miracle. The blood running out of her shoulder saturated the back seat almost immediately.

I started the chest compressions and blew into her mouth for the last time as hard as I could, so hard my eyes went blurry. I held her tight against me. Just when I was about to pull away and break into a murderous rage, she sat partway up and spit a bunch of muddy water into my face. Then she was coughing uncontrollably until her face was a brownish-red color.

I patted her on the back and smiled, holding her close to me. "Ari! Ari! Fuck, baby, I thought it was over wit' for you."

She closed her eyes and started to cry. "Jahmani, it hurts so bad. My shoulder. You gotta get me to a hospital or I'm not gon' make it," she cried.

I laid her back and put the seatbelt around her as best I could, then jumped behind the wheel and pulled away from the curb and into a rushing flow of storm water. I turned the windshield wipers on high, but it did very little to help my vision. The rain was coming down harder and harder, it seemed. The car moved slowly through the current of water. It was as if I was driving upstream. I worried I wouldn't make it to the hospital in time, that I would lose Ari before I even had the chance to have her. That scared me terribly.

"Ari! Keep talking to me back there, ma. Let me know what's good. How you feeling?" I hollered, glancing over my shoulder at her.

She licked her dry lips. "I'm in a lot of pain, but I'm okay. I'm okay, Jahmani. Long as I got you here with me, I'll be fine," she whispered, and then whimpered, holding her shoulder.

I felt sick to my stomach as I maneuvered the car off the block. Just as I was about to make a right into a river of water, I locked eyes with the big gorilla from earlier. The gorilla whose car I was driving, I assumed. He stood on the corner with his clothes matted to him because of the rain.

After we locked eyes, he took off running in the direction of the car like a crazed maniac, crashing into it so hard it rocked. "Bitch-ass nigga, get out of my car. Get out of my shit!" he snapped, punching at the passenger's window.

I stepped on the gas, the car jerked forward. The wheels spun in the water until they caught traction, then the car lunged forward into the river of water, leaving the big gorilla behind. He chased the car for half of a block, and then stopped after falling into a pool of the filthy water.

Chapter 4

I waited nervously in the waiting room while the nurses rushed Ari into the Urgent Care Unit in the hospital. I bit all my nails off and neglected to address my own wounds because I was so worried about her. My phone was flooded out. I was tired, weak, and I didn't know what to do. Every ten minutes I'd ask the front desk if she was okay, they'd give me the same answer. I was losing my mind and didn't know what else to do, so finally I sat down, and, against my will, I fell asleep.

I had to be knocked out for a few hours because about four hours after I sat down, I was awakened by a caramel-skinned older sista who looked to be in her early- to mid-forties. She had brown eyes and shoulder-length wavy hair. She was dressed in a blue pants suit with a gold detective badge on her belt. I could see her service weapon on her right side. She smelled of a sweet perfume, one that was very familiar.

After seeing her badge, I sat all the way up and wiped my mouth. "Where is Ari?" I jumped up with wild eyes.

She took a step back, placed her hand on her service weapon, and held up her left hand to calm me. "Sir, please don't make any sudden moves like that. There has been a lot going on in New York City tonight, and I am on edge. Now, my partner is with Ari. She is stable and looks to be headed toward recovery. She's awake and cooperating with my partner." She pulled out a tablet about the size of an iPhone X. "Now, we are getting our account from her, but I'd like to get your side of things. Can you tell me what happened tonight? Ari says you guys were robbed and you were beaten trying to protect her, that the perpetrators took shots at you, and she was hit. Is that an accurate account, or are we missing a few details?"

I looked at her from the corner of my eye and frowned.

"Yo, I ain't got nothing to say. I don't talk to cops. I only talk to lawyers, so if you wanna holler at me, you gon' have to holler at my lawyer first. Word up." I headed toward the hospital desk.

"Jahmani, I don't think we're done here. You need to tell me something or there's going to be a lot more investigating going on tonight, you better believe that." She walked up behind me. The scent of her perfume met me before she did. It was crazily tantalizing.

I faced her. "Yo, just let me see my goddess first. I need to make sure she's good. I ain't saying a word unless I'm able to do that." I placed both of my hands on the desk and looked into the nurse's face. "Ma'am, can you please tell me what room y'all put Ari... Ari...." Damn, I couldn't think of her last name, and I knew I'd seen it somewhere before. *Where had I seen it?* I questioned myself.

The detective walked up and placed her hand on my shoulder. "Her name is Ari Williams, and I'll take you to her. Let's go." She took off down the hallway with me in pursuit.

"Yo, how do you know my name, shorty?" I asked, catching up so I was walking alongside her.

She pushed the stairwell door open and made her way up the first flight. The tight pants of her suit conformed to her thighs all the more. "Ari told me your name. How else would I have known it?" she asked, climbing the stairs faster and faster, leaving behind her scent of perfume.

She got to the next level and pushed open the door, walked around a group of nurses, and passed the elevators just as they dinged, and four hospital staff rushed out with a bloodied man lying on a stretch. They ran down the hall with him and disappeared into one of the rooms. An older doctor ran down the hall and into the same room while a nurse ran beside him, briefing him on the new patient.

The detective waited until they ran past me before she continued on her way. She stopped outside of Ari's door, knocked three times, then pushed it inward, waving for me to follow her.

Instead of waiting for the door to open all the way, I squeezed past her and into the room. Ari sat up in the bed with an IV in her arm. Seated beside her was another black detective. She had her tablet out, typing every word that came out of Ari's mouth. They both looked over to us with eyes bucked.

I slid beside the bed next to Ari and wrapped my arm around her. "Baby, are you okay? I was worried sick about you." I hugged her to me, placing her forehead under my chin. It felt so good to have her in my arms again. I was thankful she was alive.

She nodded her head. "I'm good, Jahmani. I knew God had me. He's brought me too far to let me go like that. I was just explaining to the detective about what happened yesterday. They want to try and get this culprit off the streets." She wrapped her arm around my waist and held onto me.

I kissed her forehead and took a deep breath. "I'm just glad you're okay. I can't lose you, ma. Straight-up." I rested my lips against her forehead. The room smelled like disinfectant. There was a television hanging closer to the ceiling a little ways from her bed. It was muted.

The detective seated alongside her bed stood up. "So, you're Jahmani? How are you doing? My name is Detective Roberts. I see you've already met my partner, Detective Green. We're from the robbery and homicide division. Ms. Williams here was giving me a description of this Linx character. She says he may be a person of interest in the murder of her brother and cousin. Would you know anything about this?" she asked, looking up at me. She wore blue Prada glasses that complimented her face. She was light brown with a big nose and lips. Her eyes were brown, and her and detective Green looked to be about the same shape. She smelled like Suave powder deodorant instead of perfume, as if she'd just reapplied it.

I shook my head. "Nall, I don't know nothing about that. My concern is this queen right here, that's it. Whoever that nigga is, better be lucky he caught us off guard."

Ari adjusted her position on the bed. She looked uncomfortable. "Jahmani, they're here to help us. Why won't you just tell them what's really good?" she asked with her eyes watering.

I looked down on her and wiped her tears away. "Ma, chill. You ain't got no reason to be crying right now. You're safe." I turned to the Detectives. "I can't help y'all, miss. It ain't my job to do your work for you. Even if I did know who that fool was, I wouldn't say shit. That ain't how the game go out here in the Bronx, and y'all know it." I pulled Ari closer to me.

Detective Roberts played around on her tablet, then held one of Linx's mugshots out to me. "So, you're saying you don't want us to take this guy off the streets? I'll have you know, he has a rap sheet as long as my arm. He's dangerous, and he will finish this job. It's either you allow us to do ours, or he'll be free to finish his. What's it going to be?" she asked, looking into my eyes.

Detective Green came around the bed and stood on the side of her. "Son, I can tell you really care for Ari. I mean, she's all you've been talking about ever since I met you. If that is the case, then why won't you help us get this criminal off the streets so he can't hurt her again? Do you think it's cool for her to be looking over her shoulder for the rest of her life?" She smiled warmly.

I shook my head. "I ain't gon' let nothing happen to her

42

ever again. Son just got lucky, busting all wild and whatnot. But this ain't gon' happen no more. That's on my mother. I got Ari." I kissed her forehead and looked from one detective to the next. "Any more questions?"

Detective Green mugged me for a long time, and then shook her head. "Wow, this is the reason so many of our young black men are being killed. And why our women are being left out in these streets to fend for themselves. Here you are, thinking you are protecting this girl, when you might be the one to get her killed. That's sad," she scoffed and stepped around to the other side of the bed. "Ari, when they release you from this hospital, you need to rest up for a few days, and then I want you to call me so we can discuss this case. Here is my card." She handed it to her and looked me in the eyes.

I looked past her and turned my nose up. I wanted both of those police bitches out of the room. Even though I hated Linx's guts, I wasn't the type to get a nigga jammed up just because the streets got a little hot for me on the beef side of things. Nall. I was an animal just as much as he was. I couldn't play pussy and get them people involved. I believed in street justice, and that was the fate Linx was going to meet. Him and them Dyse Avenue Crip niggas. I would figure things out eventually. I always did. But first I needed to get my chips up. Money brought power, and power controlled the streets.

Ari took the cards from both officers and lowered her head. "I'll make sure I follow everything you guys told me to do. I really appreciate your assistance," she said without looking up to them. I had a feeling she knew I was about to come down on her as soon as they left the room.

Detective Green lowered her eyes and curled her lip up at me. She walked around the bed until she was standing in my face. "If you have any decency about yourself, you'll see to it that you really protect this girl. And by 'protection' I don't mean how you're planning on going about it. You need to help us pin this crazed lunatic before he does that same thing to somebody else. I got a feeling you know where he is and how to reach him. So, what do you say?"

Our eyes locked. I scoffed and sucked my teeth, stepped past her, and opened the hospital room door, holding it open for her and Detective Roberts to walk out of. "Ladies, it's been a pleasure. We'll be in touch." I looked from one to the other with a smirk on my face.

Detective Roberts came and walked past me, shaking her head. "Yeah, well, I guess you can't help the ignorant."

"I'll holler at you, ma. Yo, be safe out there. It's raining cats and –"

"Dogs," Detective Green cut me off, standing in my face again. She looked me up and down. "We'll be seeing you real soon, Jahmani. As soon as I find out who you really are, I'll be seeing you real, real soon." She nodded and walked out of the door, taking the knob away from me and slamming it hard.

I stood there for a moment, trying to gather myself. There was something about Detective Green that both angered and fascinated me. She seemed like she had a lot of heart, but at the same time she was real feminine, yet assertive wit' it. I could only imagine she was going to wind up being a serious problem for me. I shook my head.

"Jahmani, I already know you're heated, and I apologize. I wasn't thinking. They caught me coming right out of surgery," Ari said while adjusting herself in the hospital bed. Her hair was all over her head. She looked stressed and a little rough, but even in this state I found her to be beautiful as only she could be.

I stepped alongside the bed and looked down on her. "Yo, that ain't how we handle shit in the Bronx. We don't fuck with the law! Are you out of your mind or something?" I snapped.

She shook her head. "No, I swear, before I knew what I was doing, I was already doing it. I wish I could take it back."

I shook my head. "Nah, shorty, shit don't work like that. You put that shit in the atmosphere, now them detectives about to go to work. That's the last thing I need right now. They know my name and shit, know who Linx is. Fuck. You been around goons your whole life, and them niggas must not've taught you shit. I mean, unless they were snitch-niggas or something. That it?" I challenged, looking into her face.

She balled up her face and sat all the way up in her bed. I could tell her blood pressure was rising by the information on one of the monitors. "Now, hold the hell up. You watch your mouth when you speak of my brother or cousin. Ain't neither one of them known for being snitches. It wasn't in their nature, so you can ice that right there."

"I can't tell. Den why you so quick to fuck wit' the Jakes?" Jakes was a term we used for the police out in the Bronx. We also called them Twelve.

"You know what, Jahmani? You're being very disrespectful right now, and it's uncalled for. I told you I apologize. I didn't mean to do what I did. You don't have to worry about me telling them any useful information. I'm better than that. But if you want me to be honest, I hope they do catch Linx and give him the bidness. It would make my day if they locked him up and threw away the key, that way I wouldn't have to worry about him every second of every day. I'm going to drive myself crazy."

"No, you not, ma. I ain't about to let nothing happen to you," I promised. Her words were angering me. I had been a protector my whole life. Now she was making me feel inadequate. I didn't like that.

"They just pulled a freaking bullet out of my shoulder, Jahmani. A damn bullet. You was with me then. You were protecting me then, and I still got shot. So, why would I not feel afraid of him? Next time he could freaking kill me. Ever think of that?"

I clapped my hands together because I was so angry. My blood pressure was through the roof. I could feel my heart pounding. "That bitch-ass nigga ain't gon' touch you no more. I slipped this time. I'll never slip again. I got you, Ari. Ain't nobody gon' hurt you ever again. That's on my mother." I paced back and forth, feeling like I was about to explode. All I saw was visions of me murdering Linx in cold blood. I saw his body on the concrete with his guts spewing out. I'd never wanted to murder somebody as bad as I wanted to murder him. I fien'ed for it.

"Jahmani, come here," Ari whispered. She fluffed her pillow and placed it behind her back. I continued to pace the floor. After she saw I had no intention of coming over to her, she repeated her request with more authority in her voice. "Yo, bring ya ass over here right now, Jahmani. Dang. I'm not gon' ask you again. I'ma rip these IVs out of my veins and snatch you up. That's my hand to God. Try me. Now, come here."

I stopped mid-pace and looked over at her, laughed to myself, and stepped to her. "What's good, shorty?"

She held up a finger and wagged it in my face. "I already told you I don't like when you call me shorty. My name is Ari."

I waved her off and was about to turn my back on her when she grabbed me by the shirt and pulled me to her. "Bring yo' ass here, Jahmani. Boy, if I get out of this bed, I swear." Her hair was sticking up wildly from the pillow. There were bags under her eyes, probably from being dehydrated.

She looked angry and fine to me at the same time. I don't think I would have allowed anybody to snatch me up like that. It had to be her, and even though it was, I was having a hard time with not smacking her li'l hand away from me. "Get ya paws off me, ma. Damn. I can hear you without all this extra shit."

She pulled me closer to her. "Listen to me, Jahmani. I know you care about me. I can tell. I ain't never seen a man get so angry when it comes to the protection of me before. I don't know why you care about me so much, but you really do." She pulled me all the way down and wrapped her arms around my neck. "Thank you."

Feeling her hot body in my arms made me feel weak and strong at the same time. I wanted to snap out because of the whole detective thing and because of what she'd said about Linx, but once she wrapped her arms around me, I couldn't get mad no more. I melted. That had never happened to me before. I felt like a wimp or something. I had to get her up off me, quick.

I tried to break our embrace, but she held on for dear life, so I caved in and wrapped my big arms around her little frame. "Yo, my word, I'ma get that nigga for slugging you, ma. I'ma take care of him for putting his hands on you, period. You're a goddess. Precious. That nigga gotta see the Reaper now."

She laid her head on my chest. "Just don't leave my side. Everybody I've ever loved has been taken away from me. I'm so scared to get attached to you, and then lose you, too. I would lose my mind. Please promise me you won't go away from me. I can't handle any more loss."

I felt a lump appear in my throat. My eyes were misty. I got to thinking about my mother and how she looked when I found her. "I ain't going nowhere, ma. I'ma hold you down. All I ask is you return the favor. Be my wiz, that's what I need." I held her tighter and fought back the tears that were threatening to sail down my cheeks. After I blinked, I couldn't hold them anymore. They escaped. I felt weak and free.

"I got you, Jahmani. I can tell you really care. I swear, I got you." She broke out of our embrace and held my face with her little hands, pulling me closer to her until our lips were touching.

Hers felt like soft pillows. They were warm and juicy. I reached out for them with my tongue, tasted the skin, then sucked her upper one into my mouth before trapping the bottom. Her tongue lashed out at me, then my lips were trapped. She moaned into my mouth. Her kissing became more aggressive. Her hand slid down to the back of my neck. She gripped it, turned her head to the side, and sucked all over my lips, moaning.

My hands, on their own volition, reached out and cupped her breasts that were naked under her hospital gown. They felt plump and oh-so-soft and warm. She moaned into my mouth and continued to kiss me like a lady in heat. Her nipples poked out at me.

I made my way onto the bed. My piece was harder than ever. It jumped up and down in my pants. I was fien'ing for her. "Ari, baby, let me just." I pulled the bottom of her gown up, exposin' the fact she was without underwear. My face went between her thighs, and I swiped up and down her sex lips with my tongue. She tasted salty and creamy. Her scent was a light hint of pussy. I yearned for it to be stronger. The lips were dark brown and juicy, trimmed and moist.

She pushed me away. "Jahmani, we can't do this. Not here, please," she moaned and raised her hips from the bed.

I opened her sex lips wide and trailed my tongue all around her clitoris, sucking it into my mouth. I needed to taste more of her cream. I needed it on my tongue. I had to have it. I made loud slurping noises. I couldn't help it.

"Un! Jahmani, stop!" She beat at my shoulders, bucked, and stuffed her kitty into my face, rotating her hips in a circular motion wit' her eyes closed. "Un! Un! Jahmani!" Her legs popped around my neck, and she pulled me into her middle.

I attacked that clit, nipping at it with my teeth, sucking it with my lips, then swiping my tongue back and forth repeatedly. Her juices dripped off my chin and ran down my neck. I couldn't breathe, but I didn't care. I need her to cum on my tongue. I needed to know I made her feel better. I licked in between her folds and felt her tense up.

"Jahmani. Jahmani!"

She humped into my face and threw her head backward just as the hospital room door opened and a white woman stepped into the room with a clipboard in her hands. "Oh my!" she gasped, placing her right hand over her heart.

I jumped from between Ari's thighs and pulled her gown down, got out of the bed, and wiped my mouth. "That's my bad. I ain't mean to. I mean. I was just."

She held up a hand. "It's okay. It's nice to see our patient is doing a whole lot better."

I looked over at Ari and saw her face was red. She had the covers pulled up to her chin and couldn't even look me in the eye. She looked adorable.

Ghost

Chapter 5

"Look, Jahmani, I know you don't want to stay here. I don't, either, but ever since they found your mother and Mardi's father's body in your car, your face has been on every news outlet in the city. They're saying you went crazy and killed both. So, until the city cool down, it's best we stay here with my cousin, Misty. She stay to herself and only been in the city for a month. I already hit her hand, so we're good for a few weeks," Ari said, looking up at me after she'd closed the door to the guest bedroom we'd be staying in. It was in her cousin Misty's basement in the heart of the Bronx.

It had been one week since my mother had been killed, along with Mardi's father. Five of those days I'd stayed in the hospital with Ari, refusing to leave her side and forgetting I'd left my mother and Mason's bodies inside of my car, parked in the back of Ari's Brownstone. The cops were all over it, and Mardi was right there amid everything, putting a hundred on ten. Exaggerating. She told the media I was a scorned lover who had gone mad and killed our parents, who sided with her.

The media blew it up, and I wound up being covered by every news outlet and newspaper in the city. I felt like my time was limited. I was a target, living on borrowed time. I had to find a way to rise above the bullshit.

Lonnie was still missing. Samantha had hit my phone twenty times over the last week. Before she could get the money to Beans and his Dyse Avenue crew, her thirsty-ass aunt had stolen it and disappeared. Now she was on the run for her life and being blamed for Chase's murder, and she'd been in the news almost as much as I had been. It was crazy.

I still had my hoodie pulled around my head. "Ma, how long we about to stay here? You know how the Jakes get down in Apple. Them pigs'll be all over this spot in no time."

She chewed on her fingernail. "We'll chill for a few weeks, at least until we can get out of the city. Once it calms down, we're out of here. How does that sound?" She stepped forward and kissed my lips ever so lightly before going in on them.

I slid my hands around her waist and slowly moved them lower until I was casually brushing them over her backside. I wanted to squeeze those cheeks so bad, but we had yet to take it there. I didn't really know where we was on a relationship level, and I didn't want to scare her off. She was making it seem like she was going to ride wit' me through it all, and if that was the case, then I wanted to go as slow as she needed me to go.

She moaned into my mouth and turned her head sideways, so she was sucking on my neck. I felt her teeth bite into me, then her lips were sucking again. She moaned, "You taste so good, Jahmani. Your scent drives me crazy." She licked along my neck.

I squeezed that ass, not caring no more. I could feel myself getting hard. I had to see what those pillows felt like, and it was everything I'd imagined. Her cheeks were soft, yet firm. Every time I released my grasp, they jiggled against my fingertips. I slid my hand all the way under her backside into her gap. My knuckles rubbed against her covered kitty lips. She kissed my lips and slid her tongue into my mouth.

I made her step back and looked into her pretty face. "Ma, what's good? Why you acting all frisky and shit?" It's not that I had a problem with it, but it was uncharacteristic of how she'd been acting ever since her and I had been a part of one another. One thing about being a killer was I learned how to stay alive by picking up on people's behaviors and habits. Anytime there was a drastic change, it threw me off, especially if I couldn't determine the reason or could see it coming.

She shook her head. "Nall, it's just that being so close to

death made me realize how short life really is. Tomorrow is never promised, so I want to enjoy today. I like you, Jahmani. I can tell you really like and care about me, so I want to enjoy the time we have together. Is that so wrong?" she asked, looking up into my eyes with her pretty brown ones. I could tell she was getting nervous, as if she thought I was looking at her as a thot or something.

I brushed her hair out of her face and smiled. "Yo, it's good. I was just wondering, that's all. And besides, I do care about you. I'm feeling you like a muthafucka, baby. Come here."

I pulled her into my arms and kissed her soft lips again. I took my big hands and cupped that ass, squeezing it while my tongue danced with hers. She moaned into my mouth with her eyes closed and humped into my front. My piece was rock hard. I took her hand and put it between us so she could feel the effect she was having on me. "You feel that, baby? You're driving me crazy right now."

She squeezed it and groaned deep within her throat. "Jahmani, I ain't gon' lie. I want you. I want us to do our thing, baby. It's all I been thinking about ever since you hemmed me up in the hospital." She unbuttoned my jeans and slid her hands into my pants, pulled out my pipe, and stroked it up and down with her eyes bucked. "Dang, baby. This is a lot, though." She pumped me in her fist, licking her lips.

My eyes were barely opened. My breathing was labored, and all I could think about was getting between them thick thighs and giving her the bidness. She was so strapped. Her caramel complexion was so creamy and perfect. Her scent was intoxicating. I wanted Ari with every fiber of my being. I needed her.

I pulled her to me and slid my hands up her short skirt, feeling around for her cheeks until I located them, encased in a G-string that left her brown globes exposed. "Ma, let's do this right now. I want this cat right here and right now."

I dropped to my knees, lifted her skirt above her waist, and ripped her panties off her with one tug. She yelped. I threw them to the floor and moved her thick thighs apart. I could smell her pussy right away. I leaned forward and sucked the lips into my mouth, sliding my tongue between the folds at the same time.

"Un! Baby, there you go again. You're about to drive me crazy again, Jahmani." She opened her thighs wider and looked down on me with glossy eyes. Her tongue ran all over her lips.

I held her labia open with my thumbs. My tongue attacked her clitoris before sucking it into my mouth. I could feel her shaking as I held her steady. One of her hands rested on my head, then she was riding my mouth, bucking into it while her thighs jiggled on each side of my face. Her juices started to run out of her, and I did the best I could to suck up every bit that exited her hole. I attacked her clit with a savage-like tempo, sucking and nipping it. My tongue flicked back and forth over and over while her cream dripped from my chin.

"Jahmani. Jahmani. I'm about to cum, baby. I'm about to cum. Oh my God. Here I go already, baby." She took two hands and forced my face even deeper into her crease, riding it faster and faster. Then she shuddered and came all over my mouth. "Uh!"

I licked and sucked, swallowed, and sucked some more. Her essence tasted like a slice of Heaven. Salty, sweet, and all kitty. The feel of it going down the back of my throat got me heated. My dick throbbed against my belly. I could feel precum dripping from the head.

Ari fell against the wall and slid down it until she was sitting on the carpet, breathing hard. "Jahmani, I ain't never felt nothing like that before. You're doing something to me. Something I can't explain." She slid her fingers between her thighs and played with her cat. I watched her fingers separate her folds, then her eyes closed.

I crawled over to her, and stuck my face back between her thighs, licking all over them, biting into the fleshiest part of her thighs, sucking like crazy. She was so thick. It was driving me nuts. "Baby, give me some of this body. I want some of this body right now," I groaned, licking her fingers as they worked in and out of her. I licked in between the cracks of her fingers, then suck them into my mouth one-by-one.

She shivered, reached between my legs, and took ahold of my pipe, stroking it back and forth. "Okay, baby. Okay." She got on her knees and stroked my pipe as fast as she could. Up and down. Up and down. Then she kissed the head and ran her tongue in circles all around it, pulled the skin all the way back, and slid him into her mouth, giving me all her heat and suction.

My eyes rolled into the back of my head. "Damn, Ari," I groaned. Then my hips were moving back and forth. I closed my eyes and imagined I was hitting her pussy, then opened them and looked into her face as she did her thing. Her eyes were closed as she breathed through her nose. The dimples on her cheeks would appear and then disappear again. She looked so fucking bad. I had to stop watching her or I was about to cum early and be embarrassed as hell. Not only that, but I wanted to cum inside of her pussy. I felt like I'd been waiting to hit that for years even though I'd only known her for a matter of months, but there was somethin' in my soul that yearned to be connected to her.

She popped me out and stroked it up and down. It was drenched in her saliva. I could smell the scent of my piece and her breath all mixed. The scent wafted up to my nose and made my dick jump.

"Baby, does that feel good? Huh?" She popped me back in and nipped my head with her teeth enough to drive me crazy, then popped me back out again. "I wanna make you feel as good as you made me feel."

She started to suck me faster and faster. I whimpered and closed my heads, took a handful of her hair, and wrapped it in my fist. "Ari. Ari. Ari. Ari. Ari. Baby. You gon'. You gon'. Aw, shit. Baby."

My hips sped up. The sound of her slurping and gagging periodically was pushing me closer and closer to the edge. I moaned. She took her hands and rubbed them all over my stomach muscles. Her sucking got tighter. My eyes rolled into the back of my head again. I had an image in my head of fucking her from the back as hard as I could with her big breasts bouncing on her chest, and I felt my cum rising from deep within me.

Just as I was about to cum, she took her mouth off my dick. "Aw, man."

She stood up and bumped my dick with her elbow. I frowned and looked over to her before looking to my right and seeing her cousin, Misty, standing ten feet away from us with her hand over her mouth. She was dressed in some tight, black biker shorts with a white tube exercise bra. Both of her nipples were rock hard on her chest. Her shorts were so far in her gap that I could make out both of her sex lips. She stood on bare feet, her small toes French-tipped.

"Oh my God, I didn't know y'all was in here doing that. I'm sorry. I just wanted to bring you this key, Ari."

She stepped into the room portion of the basement. Her eyes locked in on my dick, which was jumping up and down in the air after being deprived of its orgasm. I was so mad that I didn't even put him away. I was thinking after she gave Ari that key, we were going to finish what we'd started. I was so horny I was close to finishing myself off.

Ari pulled her skirt down and fixed her top. Her nipples were also poking through her clothes. Cum ran down her thigh and onto her calf muscle. She walked on wobbly legs to meet her cousin halfway before mugging me and pointing at my dick that was standing up at least eleven inches mad.

I reluctantly put him away, watching both women as I did so. To be cousins, they didn't look that much alike, except for their body structure. Both were nicely shaped at the top and bottom. Ari was caramel-skinned, and Misty was light-skinned. Ari's eyes were dark brown, and Misty's were as well. Ari had nice, thick, wavy, almost curly hair, and Misty's was long and curly. She looked mixed to me, and I was going to ask Ari if she was. Both women were fine, but to me Ari was still the coldest.

Misty handed her the keys. "This is for the back and the front door. If you want, you can make another copy of both so he can have a pair as well. It's cool. Um, I'ma go grocery shopping later today, so if y'all want anything, just let me know. I paid this lady $200 in cash for a $400 food stamp card, so it's good. I don't mind sharing." She laughed and two deep dimples like Ari's popped up on her cheeks. She blushed once we locked eyes.

Ari nodded. "Okay, well, we'll be up in a minute, and I guess we'll figure that whole thing out." She looked up to me and frowned. I was guessing she'd seen me and Misty lock eyes more than once.

Misty nodded. "Oh, okay then. Well, I guess I'll see you in a little while. Later, cuz."

She smiled at me, then turned and walked away with her biker shorts all in her ass. I mean, I could see both golden ass cheeks clear as day. The right one had a few stretch marks on it. Both jiggled with each step she took. She looked over her shoulder before she ascended the stairs and smiled at me. I looked off, feeling the effects of her temptations only because of the state of arousal Ari had left me in.

Ari waited until we heard the door close at the top of the stairs before she frowned and shook her head, mugging me. "What was that all about, Jahmani? Did you see something you liked?" she asked dryly, picking her torn panties up from the floor.

"Yeah, your cousin bad. I see you come from a family of beautiful women." I walked over to her to try to get something going again. I needed some relief. I couldn't afford to be left in the state I was in.

When I got closer enough to embrace her, she pushed me away with her face balled up. "Well, if she's so beautiful, then why don't you go up there and hug all over her? Ugh." She looked up at me and scoffed.

I felt offended. I honestly didn't think I was disrespectin' her at all. I didn't get why she was acting how she was. "Yo, what's good? Why you seeming all hateful and shit?"

She walked over to the couch and took a seat on it, took the remote control, and turned on the 27-inch television mounted on the basement's wall. "Jahmani, it's good. Let's just sit here for a minute and try and get on the same page." She patted the couch next to her and flared her nostrils.

My piece was still throbbing in my jeans. I needed some kind of relief. I didn't have the patience to listen to nothing until I got right. "Ari, let's talk afterwards. I'm horny as hell right now. You got me all riled up. You sitting here talking about we need to discuss something. Do we really?" I was irritated.

She crossed her thick thighs, looked at the television screen, and patted the seat next to her again. "Come here."

I exhaled loudly and slid onto the couch next to her, but

instead of just chilling, I laid my hand on her thick thigh and rubbed all over it. I slid my hand under the hem of her skirt, right onto her hot box. The lips felt wet and sticky. "I want some of this right now. I ain't trying to hear nothing you're talking about until I get right," I said, biting into her neck.

Ghost

Chapter 6

"Wait. Jahmani, just listen to me, baby. I need to tell you something about my cousin. Uh! Baby, please," she whimpered.

I opened her brown sex lips wide and slid my middle finger into her, and then my index, working them in and out of her tight fit while licking all over her neck. "I want some of this pussy, Ari. I need it. I'm so hard, baby." I rubbed my piece against her side to let her see how hard I was.

She turned around to face me and tried to push me away. "Get off me, Jahmani. Let me talk to you first, then we can maybe do something after we get an understanding. Dang! Stop."

I slid her thighs open wider and really got to fingering that box. Her juices ran out of her and into the palm of my right hand, dripping from it and onto the couch pillow, creating a round, wet stain. My tongue licked all around her neck, then I was sucking on her earlobe. "Let me get some, ma. We can talk after I get some. That's my word."

I pulled my drenched fingers out of her snatch and sucked them into my mouth. At the same time, I pulled my pants down with my left hand, lying with all my body weight on her. I needed to feel her insides. Needed to connect. I was yearning for it worse than I had ever yearned for any pussy in my entire life.

My dick popped out and landed up against her brown, puffy, leaking sex lips. They were opened wide around my body, her nails already digging into my back in anticipation.

"Jahmani! Please, just hear me out, baby. Let's get an understanding before I go here with you. My temple is special to me. It's. Uh! Baby!"

I stabbed forward. The helmet of my piece slid through her

lips and hit her clit. I was searching desperately for her opening, but she kept on moving her body from side to side to evade my insertion. It was getting me angry. "Please, Ari! Let's talk later, baby. I can listen with a clear head."

I felt my head go partway in, then she turned her hips and caused me to fall out again. I wanted to scream, I was so frustrated. I was seconds away from really taking the pussy. I dug my fingers into her thick thighs and humped forward. My head smashing her clit.

She yelped and moaned, sat up, and pushed me back. "Get off me, Jahmani. I said I need to holler at you first. Damn!"

Now I was super heated. I jumped up with my piece throbbing. I squeezed it in my right hand. "Fuck, Ari! What's good? What is so important?" I snapped, harsher than I meant to, but I was sexily frustrated. I needed some pussy bad, and it was seeming like she wasn't going to give it up. I didn't want to talk. I wanted to fuck. I couldn't help mugging her.

She pulled her skirt past her knees and looked up at me angrily. "Dang, you act like you ain't just hear me when I was telling you to stop. What's your problem?" she asked, standing up and fixing the pillows on the couch.

"Man, talk. You said you wanted to tell me something, and then we could do our thing. What's good? I'm listening." I put my dick up and fixed my pants.

She exhaled and plopped onto the couch. "Jahmani, what are we going to be to each other? We've never gotten an understanding about that, and before I give you a piece of my temple, I think it's important for me to know where we stand."

I was heated. I didn't want to have a whole-ass long, drawn-out conversation before I slid into her. I wanted some of her body right now. I felt like we could have gotten an understanding much later. "Yo, it's like I told you before, Ari. I like you. I ain't finna let nobody hurt you again as long as I can prevent it. And I want you to be my woman. That's what it is, and that's how I feel. Now, come here?" I held out my arms for her.

She looked off. "Jahmani, I'm not like those average females in the Bronx or New York, period. I'm an all-or-nothing female. I go hard for my man, and I will expect you to go hard for me as well. I believe I am a queen, that my body is a temple, and I've never allowed for just no man to climb between my legs. I've only been with two people in my life, and one barely counts because I was just a naïve teenager."

"Yo, that's cool, Ari. I'm feeling you. I respect you. Now, please let me get some. Damn!" I frowned, ready to pounce on her ass.

She shook her head. "Jahmani, I saw the way you looked at my cousin, and I saw the way she looked back at you. That girl likes you. You're a fine man, and I get that, but I need you to know I'm not cool with that. If we're going to be together, then it's going to be just you and me. I don't know if you're down with that or not."

"Ari, I ain't thinking that far into the future. I'm just trying to get past this moment. I need your body right now. I've been through a lot these last few weeks, and I feel like the only thing that'll make me feel better is some of that sexy-ass body right there." I nodded at her with my chin.

She exhaled. "My cousin is only eighteen. We went to school together, and she has this thing where she has to have everything I do, or at least a piece of it. That includes my boyfriends. We are forced to live with her for a few weeks, and I'm just worried about somethin' transpiring between you two. If you think that's a possibility, then you and I should just remain friends and keep our hands to ourselves."

I felt like I was ready to panic. I saw her pussy slipping away from me, and my throat got tight. I didn't know if I was ready for any type of relationship, all I knew was I cared about her, and I wanted to protect her by any means. I knew she was a stomp-down female, and I needed her in my corner and by my side. I couldn't stand to lose Ari, especially since I yearned for her so badly deep within my soul. "Yo, ma. I'm riding for you. You're all I see. I ain't thinking about Misty or no other female. It's you and me against the world right now. Straight-up." I pulled her up and into my arms. "I just need you to trust me. I got you, boo."

She looked into my eyes. "Jahmani, please guard my heart and treat me like a queen. I understand our circumstances, and I'm willing to ride with you through them. I got your back. If you're willing to make this official, then let's do it."

She stepped on her tippy-toes and kissed my lips, soft at first, and then more demanding. Her tongue twirled around my own. I gripped that booty and slid my hands under her skirt, kneading her hot skin as if it were dough. I sucked her neck then picked her up, making her wrap her legs around me. My pants fell to my ankles. My dick jutted upward, hard and ready.

"Baby, reach under you and put me in. Put me in now, Ari. I'm fien'ing."

She moaned against my cheek, kissed my lips again, and reached behind herself. She took ahold of my stalk and aimed the head at her opening. "Here it goes, Jahmani. Un!" she moaned, putting me inside of her.

My helmet slid past her lips and into her warmth. I could feel her stickiness, her hot breath on my face right alongside my left ear. I couldn't believe Ari was giving me the pussy. I didn't think I'd ever get it. It felt hot, tight, and smelled incredible.

I took her by the waist and pulled her all the way down on it. Her pussy swallowed me, her juices dripping off my sack and down to the carpet. She tightened her arms around my neck as I tossed her up and down over and over, higher and higher.

"Mm! Mm! Uh. Uh. Jahmani! Jahmani! It's so. So. Big. My God! My God. Damn," she cried with her face in the crux of my neck.

I gripped that ass and made sure when she fell downward that she inhaled my whole pipe. My fingers played around the place where our sexes met. Her lips were puffed out and slimy with cream. I was so deep in her womb that each time I stabbed upward, she took a deep breath and dug her nails into my shoulder blades.

"It's good, Ari. It's good, baby! This pussy. Shit! It's good, Ari. Fuck, baby!" I tossed her higher and higher, crashing into the wall with her and using it for leverage. She bounced on me like a Bouncy House, grunting and moaning louder and louder. There was a wet sound coming from between our legs along with the scent of us.

I bounced her faster and faster. "I'm about to cum, ma. Yo, this cat the bomb. I'm finna cum. I'm finna cum!" I growled and felt myself shooting off. My knees got weak. I had to crush her into the wall to prevent us from falling to the floor.

She dug her nails into my back and placed her lips on my ear. "You betta not be done. Uh! Jahmani. I feel it. Please! Please, don't be done." She humped forward and licked my neck.

I fell to the carpet with her. We kissed all over each other while her hands rubbed over my broad back and down to my ass. She dug her nails into my cheeks, then pulled me forward as hard as she could. "Give me some more! Please!" she whimpered.

I cocked back and slammed forward, implanting my dick as far into her as it could go, pulled back, and slammed into her again. Then I was working that pussy over. It queefed and made smacking sounds. My balls crashed into the crack of her plump ass cheeks. I threw her right thigh on my left shoulder and rolled my back, arching it and slamming my piece deep into her hole with a steady rhythm, loving her heat. I groaning deep within my throat with my eyes closed tight.

"Yes! Yes! Yes! Jahmani! Do me! Do me! Uh, I'm cumming! I'm cumming! Do it harder, baby! Harder!"

I threw her other thigh on my shoulder and got to fucking her like I was pissed off. Sweat appeared on my forehead. My abs were locked up. My back popped. My biceps were bulging as I held my position, digging into the juicy pussy. I could feel her walls sucking at me. They vibrated as she came and came.

I licked the sweat from her neck and hugged her in my embrace. "Baby, give me this shit from the back. Get up and bend over that couch. Now." I licked her lips and slid out of her. My dick looked to be every bit of twelve inches. There were veins all over it. Her juices dripped from the tip and slid down to my sack. I could smell her on my wand. I loved it.

She got up and slowly made her way over to the couch on wobbly legs. Once there, she placed her hands on the arm of it and bent over, spreading her feet apart. She looked back at me. "Come on, baby. I ain't scared."

Her pussy lips were slightly open, enough for me to see her pink. Her inner lips peeked just past her outer ones. It looked so sexy to me. I wanted to suck all over them from that position. I stroked my piece up and down as I walked over to her. It was greasy with her fluids. When I got behind her, I pulled my skin all the way back and lead the head back into her opening, slowly at first before slamming the last five inches home.

"Aw! Yes, Jahmani. Now, do me, Daddy. Do me good!" She bit on her bottom lip and looked back at me full of lust.

I pulled back and slammed it home again, then repeated

the process. Her cheeks jiggled, along with her thighs. Her cat sucked at me hungrily. She was so wet that I slipped in and out of her box with blazing speed. The crinkle of her asshole winked at me ever time I pulled back. I sucked my thumb into my mouth and rolled it around the wrinkles of it, then smacked her cheeks hard.

She cocked her head back. "Oh, Jahmani. What you doing? Uh. Uh. Uh. Uh." She breathed heavily.

"Throw that ass back at me, ma. Come on. I know you can fuck. Show me." I smacked her on the big thang again, making her yelp.

She moaned and popped back into my lap, took ahold of the arm of the couch, and started to twerk on me. Her pussy tugged at my piece.

I held her hips. *Bam. Bam. Bam. Bam. Bam. Bam. Bam. Bam. Bam. Bam. Bam.* Harder and harder I fucked her. I had to put my name on this pussy. I wanted this woman to be mine. I was on the run from the law and a bunch of enemies. Any hour could be my last on earth. On top of all of that, I was about to get my niece back by any means and avenge my mother's death. I also had to put a few slugs in Linx's face. Through all of that, I was going to need the security of Ari. I just needed to know I had somebody in my corner who really cared about me. Somebody who was going to ride with me until the end. And I felt she was that somebody.

Of course, I could never fully know until I exposed the fact that I had killed her brother and took part in her cousin's murder. I feared revealing those truths, but the man in me knew she deserved to hear them.

She grunted and popped her back harder, really riding my dick now. The scent of her pussy was heavy in the air. I was trying to inhale it and hit it hard from the back at the same time. Her booty was shaking like Jell-O from our contact. It was a sight to see and had me on the verge of cumming. I sped up my pace and slid my hand between her thighs, pinching her clit, squeezing it like a berry.

"Uh, Jahmani. I'm cumming. I'm cumming! Oh my God! Oh my God! Yes, daddy! Yes!" she screamed and threw her body over the arm of the couch, her face in the pillows.

I was close myself. I was moaning just as loud. My eyes were closed, but when I opened them, I saw Misty sitting on the stairs with her thighs spread wide and her hand down her biker shorts, moving fast. One breast was exposed under her sports bra. She pinched the nipple and continued to finger herself, bucking off the stairs into her fingers.

The sight was too much for me. I took a hold of Ari's waist while I watched Misty and pounded her out like an animal. I clenched my teeth together and long-stroked her from the back.

Misty pulled her shorts down to her knees and really started to get it in. She threw her head back and opened her mouth wide, then got to shaking uncontrollably.

She pulled her hand from between her legs and rushed up the stairs. My last sight was of her pulling her shorts over her thick, golden ass cheeks.

I continued to fuck Ari, looking down at her to see if she noticed anything, but her face was in the pillows, moaning loudly. I slid my middle finger into her back door and came harder then I had before.

Grabbing her waist, we fell to the carpet together. She rolled on top of me and laid her head on my chest. We were both out of breath and winded. I could feel her heart beating against my chest while I rubbed all over that big booty. I still couldn't get the image of Misty out of my head. I wanted to tell Ari what happened but decided against it. I didn't want to ruin a good moment. I had five hundred dollars to my name

A Bronx Tale 2

and couldn't afford for them to get into an argument until I could get my chips all the way up.

She sat up and looked down on me. "Damn, Jahmani. You wore me out, baby. I don't know what else to say. I feel so good, though." She rubbed my chest and laid back down on top. Her tongue swiped at my nipple. "I wish you weren't on the run. I'm so scared to fall for you, and then you get ripped out of my arms. I can't take anymore death or losses, baby. I just want to be loved for the rest of my life." She kissed my chest and rubbed my shoulder.

"I know how you feel, ma. I ain't gon' roll over and let nobody kill me, though. It's gon' be a task. And as far as those pigs go, they gon' have to kill me, too. I ain't going down without a fight. Nah mean?" I squeezed her ass and felt my cum leak out of her pussy. It dripped onto my pubic hair.

"That's what I'm so afraid of. I'm afraid of you dying. If they locked you up and put you in prison for the rest of your life, I could deal wit' that. I'd hold you down. I know that without a shadow of a doubt, and I haven't even known you that long, but I can tell your heart is pure. But if they killed you, then I would lose you forever. That's what I fear."

"Yeah, well, let's stop talking all this negative shit, anyway. I ain't going nowhere. I'm about to hit up these slums, get my paper right so I can get us right. Then I'ma holler at those fools who did my moms in. At the same time, I recover my niece. Nah mean?" I squeezed that juicy booty again. I still couldn't believe how strapped she was. She was only nineteen. Most of the girls in the Bronx who were strapped were well off into their twenties and had at least one kid, so that was blowing my mind. And Misty appeared to be the same way already.

"Wait, so you're about to go out there and hustle?" She climbed off me and stood up with a frown on her pretty face.

She picked her skirt up from the carpet and stepped into it.

Cum oozed out of my head and dripped to the carpet. "How else do you expect me to get my scratch right? We gotta get the hell out of New York, and we can't do it on five hundred dollars. That's all I got to my name." I grabbed some Kleenexes from the box of them on the table and wiped my piece's head, pumping my stalk to get as much nut out of it as possible.

She pulled her top over her head. "Jahmani, if they catch you in those streets, they're going to either gun you down or take you in for the rest of your life. You do not stand a chance out there. You're all over the news. Now, I understand you only have five hundred dollars, but I have over $100,000 in my trust fund. I've never touched a penny of it, but seeing the circumstances, we may have to. I don't want you in those streets. Please listen to me."

I got dressed and slid my feet into my Jordans. "I ain't never had nobody who reached for me. I've done everything on my own ever since I was a kid. I'd feel like a straight punk if I had to depend on my woman to support me. It's not in my nature." I was born and bred by the gutters of the Bronx. I'd been trappin' ever since I was a youngin'. The thought of me having Ari support me like I was a child or something made me sick to the stomach. I couldn't see it, and I couldn't settle for that. If the world wanted me dead, then they was going to have to come and kill me, because I wasn't about to lie in wait like a fucking coward. I was a man before anything.

Ari carne over and pulled me to the couch. "Baby, things are different now. I got you. Why won't you just let me have you until we can get in a better position? It doesn't make you any less of a man if you lean on your woman. In fact, it makes you more than a man, because you have serious pride issues. I can tell." She placed her hand on the side of my face.

I lowered my head. "Yo, I appreciate all of that and everything. And I know you're genuine, but I gotta do me. I gotta get us right. It's the only way I can feel like a man. I'm sorry, goddess." I kissed her on the forehead and stood up.

She jumped up as well. "So, what are you going to do?"

Misty came down the stairs and blushed when she looked into my face. She walked over to Ari and handed her a cell phone. "It's Aunty Joyce, Mach's mother. She wants to talk to you. She say she's losing her mind."

Ari took the phone and held it to her chest. "Okay, but can you give us a minute. I gotta finish up something here with him. It's important." She looked up to me, then back to Misty.

"Aw, okay. Well, just bring my phone up when you're done."

She made her way out of the basement with both of us watching her. I noticed she smelled like a hint of kitty. I had a nose for it. I felt stirrings below my waist and tried to get her scent out of my mind. I was already feeling some type of way about Ari and having weird thoughts about her cousin was bogus.

"Baby can we talk about this after I get off of the phone?" She had put it on mute.

I nodded. "Yeah. You g'on 'head and handle your bidness. I need some fresh air." I made my way out of the basement.

Ghost

Chapter 7

"Kid, why the fuck would you risk this? Yo' ass is all over the news." My big brother, Pacho, said while looking through the glass at me. He'd been waiting on Riker's Island for almost a year to be sent to the prison where he'd ultimately serve his five-year sentence.

The dreadlocks on my wig felt itchy grazing over my cheeks. I had a big, fake beard on as well. It was the best I could do in order to get through the doors of Riker's to see him. With the get-up on, I looked just like our uncle Max. "Son, I needed to see you. I need to bust a few moves so I can get my chips up. They got me boxed in, so I gotta get the fuck out of New York."

Pacho had long dreadlocks that fell to his waist. He was Puerto Rican and black, just like myself. He had grown a beard, but it had patches in it. His hair didn't grow the way it should have. "Kid, I'm hearing that our moms got whacked, and they're blaming you for her death. I know that ain't the truth, though. Right?" He looked around and leaned closer to the glass.

I shook my head. "Nah, son. Your baby mother got our queen, along with your daughter, in some bullshit with them Dyse Avenue Crip niggas. I guess that fool Chase raped her, and she wound up knocking son's head off, then robbing the Crips for their loot and work. Them pussies retaliated by hitting our moms and snatching Lonnie. I gotta clap back at them niggas and get her back before it's too late. But in order to do so, I need some money and weapons."

Pacho lowered his head and shook it. "Them bitch-ass niggas. Kilt my momma. Took my daughter. Blood, I been hitting 'em up in here every chance I get. Me and the homies. Anything repping blue getting that metal in their throat good.

73

That's on my kid." A tear ran out of his eye. He wiped it away and exhaled. His breath caused the window to fog up. "Yo, if you serious about doing ya thing, I got a few li'l moves I can put on ya mental. But you gon' have to be quick and roll out to Harlem. One false move and son an' 'em gon' blow yo' shit back with no remorse. Nah mean?"

I nodded. "How much cake we talking?" I situated myself on the metal stool that had my ass hurting already. I knew it was all by design. The people who ran the prison industry tried to make it hard on the visitors so they could give up on their loved ones. Once a man was left behind and lost all of those who cared about him, he was prone to reoffending. He'd keep coming back to the prison until, ultimately, he stayed there for the rest of his life. It was crazy.

"Yo, it's about fifty gees and five birds of cocaine. I know for a fact it's there because I got one of my li'l hos in place. I was gon' send one of my li'l homies through there once I found one I could trust, but you're my brother, and you're on a mission. It's my duty to get you right. Nah mean? Just send me five bands when you get your hands on the scratch. Keep the yayo and the rest of the cash and find my daughter, kid. Word-up, I ain't been able to sleep ever since I found out about our mother. That bitch Samantha been out here twice before they put her on the news. She was crying and shit. Like that's gon' solve a muthafucking thing. My word, son, when I get out of here, I'm knocking her head off her shoulders. I'ma be a single father, Blood. That's on everything. I should have never nutted in that trifling bitch. I love Lonnie, but I hate her moms, son." He leaned into the glass again. "Yo, I'ma have my mans drop you off a duffle bag with some materials in it. Guard your chest, son. These streets ain't right. Them white folks get you behind these walls and it's over. Nah mean?"

I swallowed the lump in my throat. I missed my big

brother, especially at a time like this. He kept on making facial expressions that made him look just like my mother. That was hitting me hard in the heart. "Yo, I miss you, Dunn. I wish you was out here wit' me right now, B. I feel like I'm all alone. Just me against the world, kid. You know that bitch-nigga Linx tried to take my head off a few weeks ago?" I asked, feeling my eyes watering. I didn't know why I was feeling so emotional, but I was. I was missing my mother, Lonnie, and my brother. I needed my family back. I was aching.

"What? Fuck he trying to kill you for?" he snapped. His fists were clenched tight. The mug on his face was murderous.

"Kid got to wilding out and tried to choke out this dame in front of me. But before that, son tried to short me on a move we pulled together. We hit for five hundred bands and son tried to piss on me with just twenty. I wasn't having that. When I said something to him about it, he got vexed, and a li'l while later he wound up squeezing his trigger at me. Luckily, it was empty. Long story short, I wound up beating the fuck out of kid and keeping all the money. Then Mardi hit me for it. Shit been wild as hell, Dunn. My word." I shook my head again.

He pulled the hair on his beard. "Yo, I got the 4-1-1 on kid. I know where he lay his head and everything. If son trying to knock off my li'l brother, then he gotta feel them hammers. Let me know how you wanna proceed. I can send the mob at him, or I can give you all the details and let you handle your business. It's all up to you."

I wanted to murder that nigga Linx myself. I needed that kill under my belt. I didn't want nobody else handling my business for me. "Yo, I'ma come for that information, Dunn. I wanna be the one to hit kid up. Word is bond, son would've knocked my noodles out if there had been any bullets in his gun. So, it's only right I be the one to send him to the Reaper."

"Fuck, I wish I was out right now, kid. Yo, we'd handle

our bidness together and make muthafuckas kiss our asses before that steel got emptied. I miss bucking shit down."

One of the guards came past him and held up five fingers to indicate there was five minutes left on our visit. My stomach turned upside down. I felt like throwing up. I was missing my brother already. "Yo, hold ya head in there, money. You already know I'ma keep reaching. My word, you'll have that five bands the morning after I handle my bidness. I love you to death, Pacho."

He wiped a tear from his cheek. "Damn, li'l brother. You always gotta hit me with that sappy shit. How the fuck we supposed to stay killers if we're all emotional and shit, kid?" He smiled and another tear slid out of his eyes.

I shrugged my shoulders. "I don't know. I am what I am, though."

***

I received everything my brother said I would three days after our visit.

The night of the Harlem hit, Ari tried to do everything she could to keep me in the house short of tying me to a chair. That night we got in our first official argument. It started when she caught me sliding my Timbs on my feet. She walked up and grabbed the one I had yet to put on and put it behind her back.

"Where do you think you're going, Jahmani?"

She was dressed in some pink boy shorts that were all up in her crease and a matching beater that made her breasts look perfect. It took all the willpower I had in me to not snatch her up and knock that pussy down. I had a stirring for it, too. Her toes were painted pink as well, and they looked so good.

"Ma, I already told you I had to handle some bidness tonight. I gotta get a move on. Time is money. Get me that." I reached for the Timb again and she held it out of reach. I got irritated. "Yo, stop playing, shorty, before you get me vexed."

She frowned. "I don't care. I can look you up and down and tell you're on some bull crap. You're rocking a black hoodie over black pants. You got those leather gloves on your hands, and these black Timbs I guess are supposed to complete your ensemble, huh?"

She patted my waist. I swatted her hand away, but not before she could feel I was rocking two .45s with extended thirty-round clips. "What are you on, Jahmani?"

I tried to snatch my boot out of her hand when I thought she'd let her guard down, but she was way too fast for me. "Yo, I already told you I had to handle some bidness tonight. I'm finna go bust this move, then be back, and we can move forward. I ain't feeling right just sitting around all broke and shit. I gotta get my hands on some paper, then I'll be able to focus. That's just how it is. Now, give me my boot."

She held it out of reach once again and scoffed at me. "You ain't gotta go out there and do none of that. I told you I got a lot of money in the bank. Why we can't live off that until things die down? You're not making any sense, baby."

She walked toward the back of the basement where our bed and television was. Her panties were all in her juicy booty. Her thick thighs seemed to vibrate with each step. Ari was a bad woman, and only nineteen years old. I didn't think I could ever get tired or used to looking at her. She was that fine to me.

"Baby, look, I know you care about me and all of that, but I gotta handle my bidness. I gotta reach for my brother and all of that. Plus, I ain't about to sit around and mooch off you. Every second I'm in this house with nothing but chump change in my pocket, I feel more and more like less of a man. Straight-up."

She shook her head. "But you shouldn't feel like that,

Jahmani. Both of us understand what the situation is. I know if half of New York wasn't out looking for you, you would go out there and make a way. But they are, baby. You're a target right now. Public enemy number one. And we have to be very, very smart. Why can't you just let me hold you down like I'm supposed to? At least until this pass? Don't you trust me? Aren't we in this thing together?" she asked with her face turning into a scowl.

I looked at the clock and saw it was almost eight o'clock. If I was going to get all the way over to Harlem before ten, I needed to get a move on. I still had to find a car. On top of that, it was raining like crazy outside. We were on the ass-end of Hurricane Florence, so it wasn't as bad, but its presence was still felt. "Yo, I trust you, ma. I know you're riding beside me and all of that, but I gotta do me. I can't lean on you like that. I'm a man. It's my place to take care of you. Now, give me my boot, shorty. Damn." I reached for it.

She threw it to the floor as hard as she could and sat on the couch with her face in her hands. I couldn't tell if she was crying or not. Her legs were slightly parted, enough for me to see the indentation of her sex lips. I didn't know why I was peeping all of that right now, but I couldn't help but notice it. I think I was too infatuated with her or something.

"Jahmani, if you leave this house tonight, then I'm going with you. It's as simple as that." She took her hands away and I saw her eyes were watery. She wiped her eyes and rubbed her hands on the scarce material of her shorts.

I picked my Timb up and slid my foot into it, knelt, and tied it just enough. "Nah, shorty. I'm on some dangerous shit. I ain't about to have you out there like that. I'll be back in a few hours. I'll be good then. Just trust me."

Her head snapped back. "Trust you? Trust you? Why the hell should I trust you, Jahmani, when you don't trust me?

Huh? What kind of sense does that make?"

She paced back and forth and shook her head. Her lips moved but I couldn't hear what she was saying. I could tell she was heated though. She couldn't even look at me.

"Jahmani, I swear, I have already gone through this type of stuff with Mach and Mikey. I feel like it's Groundhog Day. This isn't cool. So, if you're leaving this house tonight, you're taking me with you, or don't come back at all. Those are your options, and I'm serious."

I felt offended. "Man, now you trying to threaten me. You know this the only place I got to lay my head for the moment, and you're basically saying if I don't do what you want me to do, then you're going to kick me out. Really, shorty?" I mugged her and felt my blood pressure rising.

"I'm not saying it like that. I just want to be with you. That's all. I don't want you out there in those dangerous streets without me being by your side. Stop taking offense to everything. We are in this thing together. That may not be my face on the news, but as long as it's yours, it's mine. I'm riding with you until the dirt. Now, don't deny me from being beside you." She walked over to me and took ahold of my hand.

It was something about this woman that just made me so weak for her ass. I didn't know how she could have such an effect on me in such a little amount of time, but the fact of the matter was I was weak for her. She had me feeling some type of way, and I couldn't deny it. I didn't want her out trapping wit' me this night. I knew she could be seriously hurt, and if she was, then I would never be able to forgive myself. She was already suffering from the pains of a gunshot wound to the shoulder. Had anything worse than that ever happened to her, man, I knew I would lose my mind.

But then there was this part of me that liked the idea of having my stomp-down bitch by my side. Having that female rider, being able to handle my bidness, and then my woman being right there, waiting in the car for me to return. She'd step on the gas and we'd get up out of there.

I knew I could get a lot further with her behind the wheel. All it would take is for the police to pull me over one time, and my life could be ended. I would already be driving a stolen car. The police could easily run the plates, have it come back stolen. They'd approach the car and recognize me as a fugitive wanted for murder, freak out, and gun me down. They'd probably get away with it simply because of what I was wanted for. So yeah, all of this was running through my head while she was begging me to come along for the ride.

She stepped into my arms and forced me to wrap them around her. "Baby, I don't care what you're saying. I'm coming with you. I need to be there to watch your back. Now, I'm telling you that you don't have to do whatever you're getting ready to do. I'll hold you down with all I have. But if you insist of getting your own money, then I'll have no other choice than to respect that. But I'm going. So, let me get dressed." She stood on her tippy-toes and kissed my lips.

Stepping out of my embrace, she opened the drawer and took out a pair of black pants and a black sweater. I watched her slide them on. I didn't even know what to say to her because I had so many things going through my head.

After two minutes of watching her get dressed, I got to imagining some crazy scenarios where she came out hurt, and it snapped me out of my zone. I took both pistols from my waistband and got into her face. "Shorty, you see these muthafuckas? Huh? You see this shit? The reason I got these pistols on me is because nine times out of ten I'm about to go kill up some shit. That means lives will be lost, and I don't give a fuck because I need everything these niggas gon' be holding. I don't want you around this shit. My job is to protect you from danger, not bring you closer to it. I care about you, Ari. You're like my baby and all that shit, ma. If something happened to you again, I would lose my fucking mind. I'm not kidding. I'll be back in a few hours, and I expect you to be waiting for me because, as crazy as it sounds, I know I need you."

My heart was pounding in my chest. I couldn't believe I'd just said that last part to her. I'd never said that to any female in my entire life. She was the first and only. I felt emasculated. Soft. Like a wimp. I wished I could have taken those words back, because now I couldn't look her in the eyes.

She hung her head and took a deep breath, looked into my eyes, and smiled. "Jahmani, I know what kind of man you are. I know what's going on in your life, and I'm riding with you. If you're about to ride out on somebody, then I'm going to be right there beside you. That's my place. I made that decision in the hospital, and I'm sticking to it. Can't nothing but death keep me from you. I know I'm not like the females you're used to dating, but I'ma show you different. I see the way you look at me. No man had ever looked me over with such caring and loving eyes." She hugged me again and laid her head on my chest. "I don't know how much time we got on this earth, but as long as we're riding for each other and we die beside each other, it doesn't even matter. I mean that." She hugged me tighter.

I felt so emotionally weak that I was struggling with my words. I had never heard anybody speak like that to me. I rested my lips on her forehead. "Baby, I'm crazy about you, but those words are pushing me over the edge. Yo, I'd die for you right now, ma. I need you, Ari, and I've needed you since day one. I didn't know then what I know now, but there was something in my soul that called out for you. I'm just glad I listened." I held her face in my hands and looked into her eyes.

"Baby, the mission is for fifty thousand dollars in cash and a few kilos of cocaine. From that fifty gees, I gotta make sure I hit my brother with five of them. The dope and the other forty-five thousand is mine. We about to be out in Harlem, and nine times out of ten I'ma have to buck the nigga down for this bread and dope. If you come along for the ride, you're going to be an accessory to murder. That's a felony, and you could get up to twenty-five years in prison if you're found guilty of it. With all that knowledge, Goddess, are you still willing to ride beside me on this mission?"

She smiled and looked into my eyes. "Without a shadow of a doubt. You're my man, and I'm ready to battle against the world that is against us. Where you go, I'll go." She kissed my lips and slid her tongue into my mouth while I squeezed all over that big ol' round thang on her lower back.

Chapter 8

Ari pulled along the curb of Jenkins Tavern and cut the ignition of the car. She popped the collar on her black spring jacket and rubbed the creases out of the black bandana around her face, below her eyes. She glanced over at the tavern. "Baby, it don't seem like nothing, but old people rotate in there. You're sure this is where the lick is supposed to be?" she asked with very little faith.

I pulled my hood further over my face and cocked back one of my 45s. "Yeah, my brother explained this li'l spot to me through-and-through in this kite he sent. This the spot." I felt my heartbeat speed up. It happened every time I knew I was about to get in some serious shit. I knew how Harlem niggas got down, especially their old heads. They were stubborn. That meant in order to get that fifty thousand and dope, I was more than likely going to have to cause some sort of bloodshed.

I was ready, but a part of me was still worried about Ari. No matter how much I tried to convince myself she would be okay, nothing worked. "Baby, you remember that li'l spot I just showed you in the back alley, right? You know, the one next to that abandoned garage?" I asked this question while looking out of the passenger's window at the tavern. There were a few older cats standing outside of it, smoking cigarettes and laughing all loud. While they laughed, they scanned the area as if on high alert.

"Yeah, baby, I remember. Why? Do you want me to go and park the car in that garage or something?" She looked out of the back window and then the rearview mirror. She seemed nervous.

"Yeah, but park it so your front end is ready to pull out of it, not the back. I should be back out of this place in ten minutes. If I'm not, then pull off and I'll meet you back in the Bronx."

She smacked her lips. "Nuh-uh. Hell nall, baby. If you're not back here in ten minutes, I'm coming to get you. That was the whole point of me following you out tonight. I'm on the verge of arguing with you about staying in this car right now."

I turned and grabbed her wrist. "Ari, I'm not playing. If I'm not out of this tavern in ten minutes, I'll meet you back at Misty's crib. It is very dangerous over here. Just listen to me. Please, ma." I leaned over and kissed her on the cheek, then grabbed the handle to the door, preparing to get out of the car.

She grabbed me and pulled down her bandana, kissing my lips hard, sucking them into her mouth. "Please be careful, baby. I don't want to lose you already. Please don't make me."

I kissed her lips again and nodded. "Ten minutes, Goddess. If I ain't there, roll back to the Bronx, and I'll see you in a minute."

She pulled her bandana back up and pulled away from the curb after I stepped out of the car. I watched the whip disappear down the street and turn right at the corner. The alley was just a little way from the lights, so I imagined her rolling down it and parking the car like I'd explained to her to do.

I took a deep breath and straightened my hoodie, walked up to the door of the tavern, and pulled it open with the two old heads looking me over suspiciously. I nodded at them in a 'what up?' fashion and kept it moving. When I stepped into the tavern, I was met by the sounds of the Isley Brothers' "Groove With You." The tavern only had about nine patrons inside it: six dudes and three females. They all looked to be in their upper forties or early fifties. It smelled like cigarettes and alcohol. The place was dimly lit, with a bar to the left of me and a jukebox and five pool tables to my right. Two of the dudes were throwing darts while one of the females was dancing by herself, holding her glass of dark liquor in the air and singing along to the song bellowing out of the jukebox.

The bartender was a heavyset male who looked about fifty. He had a gray afro that was bald in the middle. He draped a dirty towel over his right shoulder and held a remote control in his left hand. He flipped on the television and nodded at me. "What's up, young man?" He eyed me closely. "We don't allow no hoods in here. This is a neighborhood joint. Everybody know everybody. There is no reason to hide." He moved closer to the center of the bar and placed his hand under it. I knew that meant he was seconds away from grabbing whatever weapon he kept hidden there. This was New York, after all. Everybody was packing something.

I lowered my hood and slid into one of the stools at the bar. "That's my bad, big homie. It's still drizzling outside, that's all."

I looked around the bar and saw the other patrons were watching us very closely. They appeared nervous and uneasy. That made me feel some type of way. I was already thinking there was way too many witnesses to do what I needed to do. Then again, I was already wanted for so much shit that the judge couldn't give me any more time than he already was going to. My mind was spinning like crazy. I had to get a move on.

"So, what can I get you, son?" the bartender asked, placing his big hand on the counter.

"Yo, let me get a shot of Hennessy, dawg. No ice." I slapped a five-dollar bill on the table and slid it across to him.

He picked it up and turned his back to me, preparing my drink after putting the money in the register. It took him two minutes to make it, then he was standing on the other side of the bar, looking down at me. "So, what brings you out here to party with us old folks tonight?"

Though this may have seemed like a casual question, I knew it had a purpose. He was trying to feel me out, trying to see why I'd stepped foot into his place tonight. "Yo, I'm looking for Keeko. Pacho sent me through to handle some bidness for him. That's why I'm here." I took the shot of drink and tossed it back. The harsh liquor burned my throat and warmed my belly. I hadn't had Hennessy in a long time, so the liquor didn't waste any time giving me a buzz. It coupled with the painkillers I'd already consumed.

"I know who Pacho is, but I ain't never seen your face before. Who the fuck are you to be asking about Keeko? What's your name?" He took a .44 Desert Eagle from under the counter and put it on his waist. He made a big display of flashing it and everything. This made four of the nine patrons grab their coats and head for the exit. They looked worried.

I scoffed and mugged this big buffoon. "My name is Jahmani, from the Bronx. Pacho is my brother, and he sent me to handle business on his behalf. That's what it is. Now, are you Keeko?" I glanced at the clock over his shoulder. It had been four minutes since Ari pulled away. I had to be out of there in three more because it would take me two or three to make it to the garage.

The bartender mugged me and turned his head to the side, sucked his teeth, and laughed. "Attention! Attention, everybody. My place is now closed until tomorrow. I got some business I need to take care of. Everybody get the fuck out," he hollered.

One-by-one the remaining customers grabbed their jackets and headed for the exit, grumbling under their breaths. It took less than a minute for them to clear out. Once the last one stepped out and the door closed behind her, the bartender pulled his .44 from out of his waistband and slammed it on the bar. "I ain't heard from your brother since he got sent up the way, so it's blowing me that he would tell you to come over to Harlem all the way from the Bronx to do business with me. He should know I don't trust you rodents like that."

He spat, and some of his spit got on my cheek. This disgusted me so bad I almost threw up in his face. His teeth were yellow and jagged. His breath smelled like shit when a nigga'd been holding it for a few hours.

"Yo, I don't know what you talking about. But," I upped both of my .45s as fast as I could and placed the barrels on his forehead. "Bitch-ass nigga! I know you got about fifty gees in your office in that mini-safe behind the door. You gon' take me to it, hand that over, and I'ma be on my way. Nah mean?" I cocked the hammers.

"Shit! I should have known." He held his hands at shoulder height. "Awright, li'l daddy, ain't no reason for bloodshed. You already know what's here, so let's just make it happen. My office is this way. Follow me."

I hopped over the counter and wrapped my arm around his sweaty-ass neck. He smelled like funk and over-used deodorant. His breath smelled so bad up this close and personal that I tried to breathe through my mouth, but then I tasted it and kept gagging. I was trapped, because I wasn't letting his bitch-ass go. I didn't trust him. "Hurry the fuck up, old head, or I'ma be forced to stank yo' funky ass. Word-up."

He gagged from my arm being around his throat. "Awright, man. It ain't gotta come to that. Just take my money and leave."

We made it to the back of the tavern. There was a short, well-lit hallway with two doors along it. One said restroom, and the other said Keep Out. This was the door he stopped in front of. He took a key out of his pocket and fit it into the lock that was connected to it, opened the lock, and pushed the door in. The light to his office was off. He swiped for the light switch and illuminated it. Inside of the tiny office was a desk with a laptop computer and a bunch of papers all over it, a leather chair, ten bottles of Moet along the floor, and a steel filing cabinet that stood about six feet.

"Bruh say that muthafucking safe is behind this door." I opened the door all the way and kicked at the wall until a piece of it fell onto the dirty rug, exposing a rope that looked like a handle. "Hell yeah, there it is right there, Dunn. Pull that muthafucka out. Time is money." I flung his big ass to the floor in front of it.

He fell to his knees and bumped his forehead on the wall. He shook his head as a trickle of blood slid down his face. "Man, you Bronx niggas can't be trusted. I knew I should have never been fucking with Pacho's ass." He pulled the mini safe out of the wall and proceeded to enter the code.

I kicked him in the ass just a tad bit. "Hurry the fuck up, old head. The sooner you get me this money, the sooner I'll be out of your hair. That's my word, Dunn."

He wiped the blood from his face and looked at it smeared on his hand. "Aw, and you busted my shit. A'ight, nigga. You gon' get yours, pa. Word is bond, I ain't laying down after bloodshed." He opened the safe and began to take stack after stack out of it. He placed it on the floor next to him. "Take my money. Take all this shit. I don't care. But you gon' pay for this shit. If you don't, Pacho will." After that he continued to mumble.

"Yo, put that shit in that wastepaper basket right there and wrap it up for me. Put that dope in there, too, nigga. I want it all." I kicked the garbage can so it could be a little closer to him.

He reached for it on his knees and pulled it next to the safe, loading the first bundles of money into it. "You gon' get yours, B. Mark my words. We gon' tear the Bronx up looking for you, kid."

He continue to shoot threats my way that were heating me up. After he made me lower my hood, I knew I was going to kill him right then. I had to, especially after exposing who Pacho was to me and where we were from. I didn't know why Pacho had wanted me to tell him all those things, but those had been his direct orders to do so.

"Hello? Hello? Jahmani? Baby, where are you?" came Ari's voice.

I damn near had a heart attack. I just knew she wasn't crazy enough to come looking for me on a mission. I felt so fucking stupid for bringing her along now. "Baby! I'm back here! Damn!" I snapped, holding both guns on Keeko. He continued to fill the wastepaper basket with money.

"Baby, where are you? I hear your voice, but I can't see you," Ari hollered from a distance.

"Back here, the second open door." I was so furious that I felt like choking her ass.

She appeared in the doorway a minute later. She had a chrome .380 in her left hand, her face covered, and was shaking as if it were cold in the tavern. She looked down at Keeko loading up the money and her eyes got big. "Oh, baby, I'm sorry, but it's been more than ten minutes. I was worried about you."

"Yo, I'm almost done here. Just go wait in the car."

As soon as I said that, Keeko took a kilo of cocaine and threw it into my face. It exploded and the entire office looked like it was in a blizzard. The powder went up both my nose and mouth and left me choking before he tackled me over the desk and tried to straddle me.

"You bitch-ass nigga! You trying to rob me? Keeko the god!"

He brought his knee between my legs and kneed me so

hard I threw up in my mouth. The cocaine was choking me so bad I couldn't breathe. I could hear Ari gagging for air. I clutched the guns in my hands and tried to angle them at any portion of his body so I could pop his ass. The cocaine blinded me. My eyes were stinging as if they had soap in them.

"Jahmani! Ack! Baby, I can't. Ack!" Ari choked.

Keeko headbutted me in the chin and dazed me. My eyes crossed, and my grip got weak around the pistols. I dropped the one in my left hand to the floor and punched him as hard as I could muster in the jaw. *Bam.* Then I tried to fling him off me, to no avail. He was locked onto me like a leech, growling, "I'ma kill you, nigga. I'ma kill you for trying the god. Then I'ma kill your brother. This Harlem, son!"

He smacked me across the face and went for the gun, both of us struggling for it. Then suddenly, the effects of the drug took over me. I became so high I felt like I was floating on air and having an out-of-body experience. I felt him punching me repeatedly, but I was too fucked up to feel it. He removed the gun from my hand and smacked me across the face again. My eyes were bugged out of my head. I'd never in my life done cocaine, so the drug caught me completely off guard. I felt like I was running a million miles an hour. Everything felt numb. I felt strong, yet weak. I knew he had disarmed me, but for some reason I couldn't get sad about it or angry. I just didn't care. I was so confused for a second. I welcomed death. It was like death couldn't hurt me.

He pressed the barrel to my lips. "Die, muthafucka! Die!"

Boom. Boom. Boom. Boom

"No!"

Boom. Boom. Boom. Boom.

Keeko's body fell on top of me like a ton of bricks. I could feel his blood leaking out of him and onto me. The heavy scent of shit and gunpowder rose into the air.

Ari rushed over and started to beat at his back with her lone fist and the one with the smoking gun in her hand. "Get off him! Get off him right now!" she screamed, yanking him off me and to the carpet, where he landed with blood pouring out of his many holes.

She helped me off the desk. I was so high that it took me a few moments to understand what had just taken place. As soon as I did, I tried to wrap my arms around her, but missed her whole body. I wound up falling to my knees. I was fucked up. "Baby, I'm too high. I'm too high, boo." My head was spinning.

She staggered and dumped all the money and dope into the wastepaper basket and pulled the bag out. Then she helped me up and wrapped my arm around her neck. "Come on, Jahmani. We gotta get out of here."

Ghost

Chapter 9

It took fourteen hours for the drug to work its way out of my system. By the time it did, I had thrown up ten times, and my nose wouldn't stop bleeding. I had never been so high in my fucking life, nor pain-free. The entire time I was gone off the cocaine, I was unable to feel the pain from any of my gunshot wounds or injuries. It wasn't until it worked its way completely out of my system that I started to feel the agony of everything.

I slid out of the bed the next day to find Ari up and pacing the floor wit' her eyes bugged out of her head. She looked lost and in a trance. I'd never seen her look that way before. Her hair was all over the place, and she was wearing the same gear we'd pulled our caper in. She talked to herself and acted as if she didn't see me standing there looking at her, so I stepped into her path and grabbed her shoulders.

"Baby, what's the matter?" I asked as softly as I could. My throat was dry. My nostrils hurt, and my heart was pounding still.

"We're on the news, baby. Both of us. There was cameras on the inside and outside of the tavern. They got all the footage. I'm a wanted murderer." She looked devastated.

"What? Baby, it can't be." I tried to pull her into my embrace, but she pushed me away and turned her back to me. I was hurt.

"I wanted to be a model. I wanted to work as an actress in Hollywood one day. I wanted to be something or somebody. I wanted to change the world in my own way, but now I'm nothing more than a freaking murder. My life is over." She dropped to her knees and tears started to pour out of her eyes. She looked out into the distance. I could see her shaking.

I ran my right hand over my face and exhaled loudly. I

could taste that my breath wasn't the freshest. I wanted to console her, but I really didn't know what to say in that moment. I lowered myself one knee at a time until I was on the carpet, then slowly, but surely, I made my way alongside her. "Baby, don't you understand you saved my life? Had you not done what you did, I would be six feet under right now." I tried to place my arm around her shoulder.

She jumped up and ran, placed her back against the wall. "The Devil comes to kill, steal, and destroy. You're the Devil, Jahmani. I should have known you were from the first day you accosted me in church. Your intentions were for me to do the Devil's will all along, and I failed. I bit that apple of you, and now I'm being kicked out of the garden. I'm an outcast and surely will be sentenced to hell." She shook her head and hugged herself. She was freaking out.

"What? Man, if you don't stop talking that stupid shit, I'ma kick yo' ass in here," I warned. I didn't know what she was talkin' about, but it gave me shivers. I got to imagining hell and the Devil and all type of shit. I didn't mess around with all of that, and the fact she was talking that way was freaking me completely out. I walked over to her. "Ari, bring yo' ass here, ma, and stop playing wit' me."

I reached out for her. She jumped to the side and held up her guards. "No weapons formed against Him shall prosper, Jahmani. He never said they would not be formed, He just said they would never prosper. I rebuke you in the mighty name of Jesus. Now, flee! Flee from me! Flee, you devil!"

She ran at me with swinging fists, hitting me in the face, neck, and chest. Tears poured out of her eyes rapidly. She was screaming at the top of her lungs as well. I blocked about four blows, then snatched her little ass up, carried her to the bed, and pinned her down by her wrists. "What the fuck is wrong with you, shorty? You're freaking me out!"

She struggled against me. "Let me go, Jahmani. Let me go. My life is over now. It's over! I don't know what to do, and it's all your fault. You did this!" she screamed.

Misty appeared on the halfway-point of the stairs. "What is going on down here?" she asked in a concerned manner.

Ari yanked her wrists away and slid from under me, darted toward the stairs, and ran up them. "You did this to me, Jahmani. I'm stuck now. My life is over!" she cried.

Misty looked confused. She held up one finger. "Let me go talk to her, and I'll calm her down. I don't know what you did, but hopefully she's just being a drama queen."

I nodded and sat on the edge of the bed with my head hung low. I didn't know what to do or what to think. The time was 8:45 p.m. I figured I'd wait until the nine o'clock news came on to see what she was talking about.

I got up and went to shower. I felt dirty and in need of a good cleaning.

***

It had been two hours when Misty appeared at the top of the stairs, making her way down them. I was sitting on the couch, counting the money we'd gotten from the Keeko lick. I had already counted twenty-five thousand, and there was a nice bundle left. I was sure I would exceed the $50,000 mark. I had five kilos stacked at the end of the table as well when Misty stepped into the room with a concerned look on her face.

"Damn, you're doing it like this?" she gasped with eyes wide open. She sat on the couch across from me. Her shorts were so small that when she sat down, they basically disappeared. All that was left was her thick thighs. She wore a cutoff shirt that showcased her flat tummy with the pink diamond belly ring. She smelled like Prada perfume. Her feet were bare and looked freshly pedicured. She crossed her big legs, exposing the bottom portion of her left butt cheek. It looked darker than the skin along her thighs. I tried my best to not look but failed.

"Yo, what's good with Ari? Shorty finally calmed down yet?" I asked, trying to change the subject.

She pursed her lips and looked off. "Okay, don't freak out, but Ari left, like, thirty minutes ago. She said she needed to clear her head, that she'd be gone for a few days."

I jumped up and dropped a bunch of money all over the carpet. "A few days?" No, the fuck she ain't!" I threw the money I was counting onto the couch and ran to the stairs, taking them two at a time. When I got to the top, I rushed into Misty's crib and looked around. "Ari! Ari! Where the fuck you at, ma?" I opened the door to every room in the house, peeking inside of them, finding them empty. Then I opened the front door and stood on the porch. I noticed Misty's car was nowhere in sight. It felt chilly out.

My head began to hurt. I was confused. I stepped back inside and closed the door, then went back into the basement. Misty was bent over on the floor, picking the money up from the carpet. Her short-shorts were all up in her ass. "Yo, shorty, what the fuck you doing?" I snapped, rushing over and snatching the money out of her hands roughly.

"Dang, I was just helping you out. You act like I was trying to steal it or something." She rolled her eyes and got off her knees, dusting them off. Her thighs looked as if she had rubbed baby oil into them, though now her knees were slightly ashy from the carpet.

"Shorty, I don't know what you was doin'. I just met you. Paws off my scratch, though. I don't play that shit." I gathered all the money and started to recount it from scratch. Even though I couldn't visibly see any money tucked away on her,

I wasn't playin'. Every penny meant something to me because I'd almost lost my life over it.

She sat on the sofa and crossed her big legs again. "I hope you ain't mad at me because of the bullshit she's pulling. I ain't got nothing to do with that. I'm the one that took y'all in, despite your situations. That's pretty noble."

I took ten $100 bills and tossed them at her. They landed all around her. "Huh, take this li'l paper and shut up. I don't like when people throw shit in my face that they done for me. I'm a self-made nigga. I don't need nobody for shit. You just caught me at the wrong time. Word-up." I licked my thumb and kept on counting my paper. "Why the fuck you ain't tell me when shorty first left?" I looked over at her.

She knelt down and gathered up the money, then sat back on the couch, counting it. Once again, she crossed her big thighs. "She told me not to say nothing for at least thirty minutes. That's my big cousin. What else was I supposed to do other than listen?" She turned her attention back on the money in her hand, counting it bill-for-bill. At the duration, she folded it and slid it into her bra. "So, how did she get involved with such a stomp-down animal like you? You seem like you're crazy. Fine, but definitely crazy." She smiled and held up her chin with her right hand, resting her elbow on her thigh as if she were all tuned in to me.

"I got at her. I ain't never seen no female as fine as Ari. She went to my mom's church, and when I saw her, I just had to say something. She played me off as a nigga bothering her, and that got me interested in pursuing her real hard. Long story short, that's my heart right there. Even though she wilding right now."

Misty popped her head back on her neck. "Never seen nobody as fine as her? I hope that was before you met me? I mean, dang. Look at me."

She turned around in a circle and allowed me to admire her body. When she turned around so I could see that big ol' ass, I noted her shorts were all in between her cheeks. When she faced me, the material covering her gap looked molded to it. I could even smell her from where I was sitting.

I couldn't lie. "Yo, I can't front, shorty. You look good as hell, but you ain't fucking wit' Ari. I really don't like yellow hos like that, anyway. Y'all think y'all the shit when darker-skin females crushing y'all in my book. Ain't nothing like some dark skin. That's why Ari so cold."

She sucked her teeth and crossed her arms in front of her. "I don't care what you talking about, Ari don't look better than me. I know I'm bad. I mean, I ain't got a big head or nothing, but I've been told I'm flawless. That's by niggas and bitches, so bump your opinion. Shoot." She sat down and frowned her pretty face.

I licked my thumbs and kept counting my paper. "Yeah, well, I don't give a fuck what them niggas or them hos had to say about you. I'm looking at you right now, and I'm telling you Ari crushing you. You straight. I'll give you a nice seven, but you ain't getting no more than that. Bring yo' ass over here and help me count this money. Make yourself useful instead of staring at me and shit." I tossed a bunch of bills at her, forcing her to pick 'em up.

"I ain't know you was this damn rude. I thought you was one of those smooth niggas but come to find out you ain't shit but a goon. That's crazy." She picked up the money, making sure she was bent over with her ass facing me. I could see her pussy print from the back.

My dick got to stirring in my jeans. I ain't gon' even lie, this li'l bitch was super bad to me, put I wasn't about to let her know that. I still didn't think she had shit on Ari, but she wasn't as far back as I was making it seem.

"Yo, where would she go, anyway? Did she tell you? Don't be lying if she did."

She finished picking up the money and came to kneel in front of me on the other side of the table. "She probably went over my mother's house out in Queens. If not there, then probably one of her girlfriends' houses. I don't know because she didn't tell me nothing." She turned her head to the side. "Do you really think I'm ugly, though?"

I took a bundle of cash and sat it in front of her. I'd already counted it, and it came to twenty gees. I'd thrown five bands on the floor to her, so when she finished counting the total, it should have been twenty-five gees altogether. "Yo, I told you, you're straight. I ain't say you was ugly. Now count this bread for me." I pushed it over to her and laughed in my mind. She was immature, I could tell. Real vain. My comments were eating her alive and probably turning her on at the same time. It was funny to me.

"Yeah, I know you didn't technically say I was ugly, but you didn't say I was super bad, either. Is it because of my forehead? When I was real little, all the girls used to say I had a big forehead. Even to this day whenever I get into it with anybody on Facebook, the first thing they attack is the size of my forehead. It makes me so insecure, and that's what you see, isn't it?" She held the money so tight in her grip that she was balling it up.

To me, her forehead looked perfect for her face. It wasn't big at all. In fact, there was nothing wrong with her face or her body. She was a pure dime. She had some big lips, but that just made her look even colder. I was just Ari-drunk. Didn't no female look like shit compared to her. "Yo, your forehead is a li'l big, but I mean, we all got flaws."

She slapped her forehead and held her hand over it. "Dang, you ain't gotta be so honest. Don't you know females are very sensitive? Words hurt us more than they do a man."

I couldn't help laughing out loud. "Shorty, you're good. Like I said, ain't nobody perfect. Nobody."

"Shit, I can't see anything noticeably wrong with you. The first thing I thought when I saw you, was how fine you were. Then you have all those muscles and that wavy hair. That's ridiculous. What are your flaws? I damn sure wanna know."

"I get headaches real easily when bitches be whining and shit, so shut up and count that bread for me. A'ight?" I picked up a bundle of cash and got to counting beside her, thinking about Ari and praying she was okay.

Chapter 10

"Jahmani. Jahmani. Wake up and eat this food. Damn, you gotta put something on your stomach," Misty said, shaking my hip. Ari had been gone for a full twenty-four hours. Neither Misty nor I had heard anything from her. I'd even had Misty call around to her relatives, and nobody had seen her. I was beginning to worry and had only been able to eat minor bites of food.

I yawned and stretched my hands over my head. Misty stood on the side of the bed with a plate loaded up with breakfast food. She'd made French toast, scrambled cheese eggs with onions and bell peppers, Tennessee Pride hot sausages, and grits. It smelled so good that my stomach was growling like a lion trying to protect its pride.

She slid into the bed and sat beside me. "Come on, Jahmani. If you don't eat, you're going to lose all those muscles. She forked up some of the cheese eggs and held them to my lips.

I turned my head away and slid out of the bed. "Shorty, don't be trying to feed me and shit. Your cousin'll whoop your ass if she found out I'd eaten from your fork," I scoffed and yawned.

Her eyes were bucked. She looked down in the direction of my crotch and covered her mouth. "Boy, you better cover up your thang. It's all out of the boxer hole." She covered her eyes and turned away from me, all childlike.

I looked down and saw my piece was standing straight up in the air. I guess 'cause I'd just woken up, my dick was still super hard. I adjusted it and tucked him back into my shorts. "My bad. You heard anything from Ari?" I asked, taking the plate of food out of her hands and sniffing it.

She stood up. Her nipples were poking through her white

beater. Her face was flushed. She sucked on her bottom lip and refused to make eye contact with me. "Nall, she ain't hit my phone yet. I would have let you know if she did. But…. Never mind." She started to make her way out of the basement.

"But, what? Man, bring yo' ass back here before I fuck you up."

She spun around and walked back to me. "She made a status on Facebook, and one of her exes was in the background on two of the pictures she posted. I think she back fucking with him or something. I'm sorry."

I felt all the blood rush to my head. "What the fuck you mean? Go get your phone. Right now, shorty! Hurry up!"

She jogged out of the basement and ran up the stairs with her big booty jiggling. I sat the plate of food on the dresser. Now my stomach was turned upside down. I felt sick. I imagined her fucking with another nigga, and it made me want to go crazy. Ari was my woman. She'd stopped a nigga from smoking me. I owed her my life. Wasn't no nigga about to have her but me. I'd kill this other bitch-nigga. I meant that shit.

Misty came down the stairs and handed me her phone. "There is the status, and if you scroll down, you'll see a dude's face. That's her ex. His name is P.T. They fucked around for, like, two years. I think she still loves him because every time something major happens, they wind up together again. But he's a serial cheat. It won' last."

I read over the status. It said: *Sometimes you have to stop chasing the future and love your past.* I didn't know what that meant, but there were two pics of her and him hugged up. They were dated for the day before. It crushed me. I wanted to fall to my knees. I felt like I had been punched in the stomach by a heavyweight boxer. I kept reading over the status again and again, then I'd scroll down to the pics under it.

Before I knew what I was doing, I took Misty's phone and threw it against the wall as hard as I could, breaking it into a hundred pieces. Then I stood there with my chest heaving up and down. My vision was hazy. I balled and unballed my fist.

Misty looked down at the phone with her right eyebrow raised. "Uh, that's the new iPhone X. It cost me damn near five hundred dollars, and that was on discount. Are you planning on repaying me for it, or…?"

"Where the fuck this bitch nigga stay at, shorty?" I asked, looking down on her with my nostrils flared.

She waved me off and headed toward the basement steps. "No, I've said too much already. I should have kept my mouth closed. I'm not getting into that. Can't believe you broke my phone. Damn, yo' ass crazy."

She stepped her foot on the first step. I rushed and grabbed a handful of her hair, pulling her off it. I kept on imagining Ari and that nigga hugged up, trying to rekindle an old flame, and it got me so heated I felt like killing something.

"Where the fuck he stay at, shorty? I ain't gon' ask yo' ass again," I said through clenched teeth.

She yelped and struggled against my right hand that was tangled in her hair. "Let me go, Jahmani. Damn, you're ripping my shit out. Why are you taking this out on me? She's the one being a thot." She wiggled out of my embrace and wound up on the floor on her butt. Her hair was askew. She frowned and backed away from me.

"Yo, Shorty, get yo' ass up. You about to take me over there. I gotta see her so we can get an understanding. I ain't about to let her kick me to the curb like this. I got feelings for her." I felt like I was about to be choked up, so I stopped talking. I went into the bedroom portion of the basement and put my .45 on my hip, then grabbed five solid $100 bills and tossed them to her. "Huh, this for your phone. I'll give you a few more hundred when we get back. Where are we headed?"

She got to her feet, bent over, and picked up the money. "He stay in Brooklyn. About ten blocks over from Bed-Stuy."

***

When we rolled up to P.T.'s Brownstone, there were four dudes sitting on his stoop smoking blunts. Two of them looked to be in their fifties, and the other two couldn't have been older than twenty-five. I eyed them for about five minutes, trying to see if I picked up any killer vibes from anyone, and didn't. If I'da felt any of them were a threat by first glance, I had my mind set on gunning 'em down. I was that heated.

"Man, I can't believe you're actually going through all of this for Ari. I ain't never had no man this crazy about me, and I'm a good-ass girl. I've never cheated on any man I've been with. I'm loyal, I'm submissive, and besides this damn forehead, I think I'm quite attractive. I mean, I guess. But then again, you've kinda opened my eyes to let me know I'm not all that. But everybody else say –"

"Shorty, shut the fuck up. Damn, you've been talking ever since we got in the whip. I need to think. Now, sit back and chill. Fuck," I snapped and mugged her li'l ass.

She frowned and crossed her arms in front of her body. "Okay."

I stared her down for a few moments, then looked back out of the window. "Now, tell me what kind of nigga this fool is? Is he a killer? What the streets say?"

"I thought you just told me to shut up?" She rolled her eyes.

I grabbed her by the throat and put my face close to hers. "Li'l one, stop playing wit' me. Is this nigga a killer or not?" I pushed her away enough so she landed against her driver's

104

door.

"I don't know. Ari ain't never told me he killed nobody. I've only met him a few times, and each time he was trying to fuck me on the low. He don't seem like one, but he does have a bad temper. Why is that important, anyway?" she asked, rubbing her neck.

I opened the passenger's door. "Look, you stay yo' ass right here until I get back. Don't get out this car, Misty, I ain't playing. When you see me come out, you start the engine, and not before then. You got that?"

"Yeah, Jahmani. Damn, you standing on me like I'm your bitch."

"Yo, you heard what I said." I slammed the car door and made my way toward the stoop. The four men were talking at first, but when I placed my foot on the first step, they stopped and stared down at me. I put a fake-ass smile on my face and kept on. "Yo, I'm looking for my cousin P.T. I'm from Queens, and I ain't seen him in a minute. Y'all know what apartment he stay in?" I asked, looking from one to the other.

Both old heads looked off, and one of the younger cats stepped off the stoop and began to walk down the block. That concerned me. A part of me wanted to catch up to him and snatch him up, but I let him go and looked toward the rest of the men. "Anybody know?"

The last younger dude had some real nappy dreadlocks. He scratched his scalp and took a pull of his blunt. "Yo, how we know you are his cousin, B? You could be anybody," he said this with his eyes half-closed. He smelled like musk and sweat.

"Yo, that's my kinfolk. I ain't got no reason to lie. Fuck it, I'll find his crib on my own."

"Why don't you just text the god and get it from him?" one of the old men said before I brushed past him and into the hallway. It was filthy. Litter was all over the place. It smelled like somebody had just taken a strong piss. I climbed the stairs, not knowing how I was going to find his apartment.

I had made it no further than the third level when an older woman came out of her apartment singing a Mary J. Blige tune to herself. When she saw me, she jumped. "Whew! Boy, you scared the heck out of me. What are you doing up here?" She looked me over suspiciously.

"I'm looking for P.T.'s crib. I can't remember which one it is. He got some stuff for me."

She smiled. "Oh, you looking for some of that good-good too, huh? Yeah, P.T. got that sauce. I'm headed down to get me a few as well. Come on, sugar. It's alright." She waved for me to follow her. "You're a handsome li'l thang, ain't you? Damn, they didn't make 'em like you in my day. If they would have, I would probably have twenty kids by now. Child! Look! I got some stories for your tale! Come on, sugar." She started to hum to herself.

I kept on looking around for any potential predators. I knew they got down in Bed-Stuy. I'd done my share of dirt out there, and I didn't like them Brooklyn niggas. They were grimy as they came. I was still thinking about the one young dude who walked away from the stoop, ignoring me.

The older woman took me back to the first floor. She walked halfway down the hall and started to knock on apartment 1-C. She looked over her shoulder at me. "What church do you go to? You sho'd make our Deacon Board look a whole lot better. Some of them men look tired, child. Like they been working 23-hour days." She laughed to herself. "23-hour days for the last five years. And they ain't got no inspiration. I would love to see you in our church."

I wanted to tell this woman to shut up so bad. She was irritating, and she had my nerves on edge. I couldn't think straight with her steadily running her trap the way she was. But instead of snapping out at her, I simply smiled and nodded my head.

"Yo, what's good?" came a voice on the other side of the door.

"Baby, it's Pam. You know what's up, so open the damn door, boy, before I tell your mother on you." She looked angry.

"Hold on." I could hear him fumbling with the locks.

The only thing going through my mind was that I could not believe Ari was laying her head in a place where somebody was sellin' dope. It was blowing my mind and making me more and more angry.

The door opened, and some light-skinned nigga with long dreads stood in the doorjamb. There was big cloud of smoke that rushed out of it into the hallway. It was so strong I felt like I caught an instant contact high.

"Yo, Pam, I hope you got some cheese wit' you, because I ain't about to keep hitting you just on the strength of my mother. I can't pay my bills with courtesy. Nah mean?" He looked from her up to me. "Yo, who is you, money?"

Pam went into her big bra and handed him a rolled-up twenty. "You always gotta be so damn disrespectful. Get me right before my show come off commercial." He handed her a bag, and she walked away from his door. "Y'all take it easy. And I hope to see you at Mercy Memorial Baptist Church, right around the corner there. You'll give all of us ladies a reason to come and praise the Lord," she flirted before rushing up the stairs.

I looked into P.T.'s face. "Let me holler at Ari."

He frowned. "Son, you ain't answer my question. I asked you 'who are you?'" He sucked his teeth and tried to look all hard, but the only thing going through my mind was giving him a closed casket.

I was seconds away from putting holes in his face to make

it look like a bowling ball when Ari pushed him to the side and looked up at me. "Jahmani? What are you doing here?" she asked, hugging herself. There was a draft coming from outside and seeing as she was only dressed in a pair of short-shorts and a tank top, I guess it was getting the better of her. Her teeth chattered.

"Ari, what the fuck are you doing over here with this nigga?" I felt my temper getting hot, but at the same time I wanted to pull her into my embrace and hold her close. I could smell the scent of her, and it was driving me crazy. I wanted her back.

"Jahmani, I don't know what to say. I have to be here. P.T. will protect me and help me stay out of prison. I trust him. Please understand."

She tried to touch my arm. I yanked it away and mugged her, then looked over her shoulder at him. He had one of those dumbass, amused looks on his face. I wanted to shoot it off. But then again, I was taught by my mother that I was never supposed to check the nigga in situations like these. I was supposed to check the bitch. So, I tried as hard as I could to keep my comments to myself, but I was boiling on the inside.

"I'll protect you, Ari. You know I will. I care about you, shorty. I wanna spoil you for the rest of our lives. Damn, why are you doing this?"

She lowered her head and slowly shook it. "Right now, I'm doing what's right for me. I can't explain it. I gotta get my head together, and when I do, I'll contact you. It shouldn't be more than a few more days. A week, tops."

P.T. slid his arm around her neck and kissed her cheek. "Baby, you done talking to him so I can close this door? We're lettin' all of the heat out." He looked at me and smirked.

Ari nodded. "Yeah, I don't have nothing else to say right now."

She crushed my soul when she turned her back and walked off on me. I could see her sitting on the couch. Her hands covered her face.

"Yo, money, that's just what it is. She'll fuck wit' you when I'm done. Nah mean?" He sucked his teeth and laughed.

I was boiling so bad I was shaking. I wanted my woman. I needed to feel her in my arms again, needed to lay in the bed with her and listen to her hopes and dreams for the future. I missed her laugh, her voice, her scent, her caresses. I missed the sight of her perfect body, the feel of her soft skin against my own. I loved this woman. As much as I hated to admit it, I loved her.

I stepped to the side of him. "Ari, I love you, ma. Man, I love you with all my heart. Please don't do this shit right now. I need you, boo." My throat got tight again. I felt like begging on my knees. This woman had saved my life. I had been through more things with her in a month than I had with anybody else in my entire life.

Ari picked her face up from her hands and looked toward the door. "What did you say, Jahmani?"

P.T. blocked my path. "A'ight, son, she'll fuck wit' you later." Then he slammed the door in my face.

I could hear them arguing on the other side of it. I waited for five whole minutes after they stopped, anticipating her opening the door and running into my arms, but none of that happened. I left out of the hallway, crushed. I felt like my heart had been stepped on and kicked into the wall.

When I got outside, Misty started the engine. I opened the passenger's door and got in. I was so out of it that I took my seatbelt and put it around me. I was devastated.

She looked over at me and smiled weakly. "I'm sorry, Jahmani. You need to know their relationship won't last long. It never does. I give it two weeks, tops." She put the car in drive and pulled away from the curb.

I couldn't take my eyes off P.T.'s building. I wanted to burn that bitch to the ground. If I had to kill him in order to get Ari back, then I would. No man was about to take her away from me. No man. I wasn't going. I felt like I could throw up.

Chapter 11

That night I did something I had never done before. I took a half ounce of cocaine, sat it on the table in front of me, and separated it into thin lines, tooting them one at a time. I was trying to take away the pain in my heart. Every time a tear would roll down my cheeks, I'd wipe it away. I tooted the powder until my nostrils hurt. I was so high I couldn't be sad anymore.

Misty came down the stairs at one in the morning with an extra-large meat lover's pizza from Bertolli's. She knelt on the floor next to the couch and sat it down. She also had a bottle of Moet in her right hand, already popped. "Yo, I know you ain't got an appetite an' all that, but if I gotta force you to eat something tonight, then I will. You're starting to look a li'l scrawny," she joked.

She opened the box, and the scent rose to my nose right away. It made my stomach growl. She took a slice and pulled it up. There was so much cheese on it that she had to raise her arm all the way in the air before it broke. I licked my lips and rubbed my pants legs. "Yo, come here and feed me, shorty."

She popped her head back. "You're for real?"

I nodded. "Yeah, I'm hungry, and you say you got me, right?"

She smiled and nodded. "Hell yeah, I do." She got up and sat beside me on the couch, held her hand under the pizza just in case any of it fell, and brought it to my lips. "Here you go."

I opened and chomped down on it, tearing off a nice amount and chewing. It tasted so good, like the flavors had been made specifically for my palate. I closed my eyes for a second, and when I opened them, she was smiling and looking me over. She took her fingers and wiped the grease away from my mouth, sucked the remnants from her thumb. I swallowed and nudged my head at the bottle of Moet.

She got up from the couch and bent over to grab it. I saw how her boy shorts were all in her crack. Both cheeks were well exposed. She looked over her shoulder at me and laughed, then came back and held the bottle to my lips for me to drink. "Can I ask you a question, Jahmani?"

I swallowed, got enough, and moved my lips away from it. "G'on 'head." I pointed at the pizza. She took it and held it to my lips again. I could smell the perfume from her hand.

"If you'da ran into me first, would you be just as crazy about me as you are about Ari? Or is my forehead a deal breaker?"

I couldn't help but laugh at the last remark because I could see my li'l jabs at her were cutting deep to her soul. I believed all bad women had insecurities buried deep down within them. All it took was for a man to zoom in on the smallest flaw and attack it. Most niggas were so transfixed by the sight of a bad woman that they were hardly ever able to see past the beauty, but not me. I'd been around bad women my entire life. I made it my business to see what other men didn't see, except when it came to Ari. I couldn't find one flaw with her, and that frustrated me. She was so far in my system that it hurt.

"Ma, if I would have seen you first, I wouldn't have fucked with you because you are too yellow. Your forehead ain't got shit to do with nothing. If you was a li'l darker, I could look past that imperfection."

She placed her hand over it, frowned, then rubbed her skin and stood up. "Really? It ain't my fault I'm yellow. I'm mixed. My mother is black, and my father is Dominican. Dang. You ain't all that dark yourself. Shit, you gotta be mixed too, ain't you?" She placed her hand on her hip.

My face was about a foot away from her box. I could smell a hint of it mixed with the scent of perfume. Her and Ari gave off the same fragrance. I wondered if it was because they were cousins. "Yeah, I'm Puerto Rican and Black. My mother is Rican, from San Juan. That's why I'm a li'l lighter. But I ain't trying to date me, though. Nah mean?" I turned the bottle of Moet up, looking out at her.

She ran her hand over her stomach and fixed the elastic of her boy shorts, pulling them upward and molding them to her cat down below. "So, you're telling me that when you look at me, you don't feel nothing?"

She turned around and showed me that fat-ass booty. It was nice and round. The cheeks were chunky with small traced of stretch marks decorated all over them. It looked so good that I almost bit her on it. My head began to spin, and then I was suddenly woozy. My dick got so hard in my pants that I wanted to take it out. I got hot. I reached and placed my hand on her ass, rubbing it in a circular motion. "Damn, shorty."

She placed both of her hands on the table, and spread her legs, looking over her shoulder at me. "I knew you had to at least like this. I'm thick, can't nobody deny me that." She sucked on her bottom lip, looking sexy as hell.

For some reason I kept getting higher and higher. My dick was throbbing like crazy. I trailed my fingers down the crack of her ass and wound up rubbing her pussy mound. I grabbed her hips, scooted to the edge of the couch, and brought it to my nose. I inhaled it and shivered. My nose poked at her gap.

"Just let me sit on your lap, Jahmani. Please. Let me do my thing. We ain't gotta go no further than that." She stood up to face me. Her panties formed a wedgie in her pussy. She rubbed her camel toe, looking down at me. "Can I?"

I saw the way her finger stuffed the material further into her gap, and my piece wormed its way out of my waistband on its on. I wanted some of that eighteen-year-old pussy. I didn't know if I was gon' fuck or not, but Lord knows I wanted some of that box.

I nodded and handed her the bottle. "Come on, shorty. Sit that big ass in my lap." I scooted all the way back and kicked my pants off. I didn't want to think about the hurt I was feeling over Ari. I didn't want to address the fact this was her little cousin or the thoughts in my head of what I assumed her, and P.T. were doing in that moment. I didn't want to think about her, period. I just wanted to enjoy Misty's strapped ass and allow the cards to fall where they may.

She turned around with her ass in my face and pulled her shorts all the way up, exposing her cheeks. Then she slowly eased into my lap, laying her back on my chest. The heat of her cheeks seamed to sear my lap. Her ass was soft and full. She smelled so sweet and felt so light in my lap.

"Mm, now this is nice." I closed my eyes and felt my dick throbbing against her ass. "Damn, shorty, you gon' get me in trouble." I placed my hands on her thick thighs and rubbed them up and down, squeezing them. I placed my chin in the crux of her neck and rested my lips on her left ear lobe.

She spread her thighs, cocked her back, and slowly started to give me a lap dance. "Damn, Jahmani. Ooh. Baby. I can feel that pole. It's big." She rolled her back and danced faster, popping and popping. It felt like she was jerking me off.

I groaned and held her thighs, then I was humping into her ass. The liquor and the cocaine spurring me on. "Uh. Misty. Yo. Shorty. Aww, shit." I brought my hands around and cupped her big titties. I trapped the nipples between the cracks of my fingers, pulled on them, then cupped both breasts altogether.

"Go under my shirt, Jahmani. I wanna feel your hands on my skin. Please, let me feel them on there." She danced faster and faster.

I slid my hands under her tank top and played with her

titties. They were hot, the areolas huge and erect, nipples standing up nearly an inch apiece. I squeezed the mounds as they jiggled on her chest.

"Uh! Jahmani? Why can't we just?" She jumped off my lap and got between my legs, grabbed the bottle of Moet, and turned it all the way up, guzzling it. Then she handed me the bottle and pulled my dick out of my boxer hole, stroking it up and down. She stuck her tongue out and licked all around the big head, vacuuming me into her mouth and sucking hard.

I shivered and grabbed a handful of her hair. "Aw, fuck, Misty."

She popped me out of her mouth. "I'ma show you how redbones get down, and why you should be jocking us and not them dark bitches. I'm finna turn yo' ass out onto something new." She slid my dick into her mouth and sucked it until her nose touched my pubic hair, then she pulled me out and rubbed the head all over her pretty face. "I'd worship this dick. Ari don't know a real nigga when she see one." She swallowed me again and went to work, making all kinds of loud, nasty noises that were driving me insane. She rubbed her hand up and down my abs, going over the ripples of it.

I humped into her mouth. "Bitch, take them hands away. Don't pump my shit. Suck me wit' no hands. Aw, fuck! Misty!"

She took her hands away and bobbed in my lap, sucking me harder and harder. Her big breasts slapped on my thighs. She breathed hard and gagged occasionally. It felt good, I couldn't lie. It felt so good I whimpered deep within my throat.

She removed her head and rubbed my helmet along her teeth, sending tingles through me. "Cum in my mouth, Jahmani. Let me swallow that shit. Come on!" Her mouth covered me again and got to going berserk. Up and down, up and down. Her tongue flicked up and down my pee hole.

It became too much. My toes curled. I felt weak, and then I was cumming while her teeth nipped at the skin of my helmet ever so lightly. "Uh! Misty! Fuck!" She started stroking it with her right hand, making me cum harder and harder. I could feel the globs shooting out of me.

"Mm. Mm. Yes." She swallowed all of me and took my dick out of her mouth, kissed the head, and licked up and down it all the way to my balls, sucking both into her mouth, licking under them, and venturing her tongue into the crack of my ass. That made me jump. I reached over her back and smacked her on her cheeks hard.

She yelped and licked my stomach. "You wanna spank me, Jahmani? Huh? You wanna treat me like your little girl?" She slid her boy shorts down and stepped out of them, then ran her hand between her slit while she stood in front of me. She got on her knees and bent over. "Come spank me, daddy. I know you want to. Spank me right now. I need you to." She held open her ass cheeks and licked her lips.

My dick was super hard and leaking. I got down on the side of her and smacked that ass again. It shook. She whimpered. I grabbed her around the waist and slapped it five hard times in a row, then slid my fingers into her oozing gap. Her essence dripped out of her and down her thighs.

"Spank me, Jahmani. Take your anger out on my ass. Please. I want it so bad. I'm Ari! I'm Ari!" she hollered.

That sent chills through me.

She got up and bent over the couch wit' her hand between her legs, playing with herself. "Come on."

I sat back on the sofa, pulled her over my lap, and got to spanking that ass for a full minute. Hard, too. Her cheeks jiggled and turned red. I could smell her pussy getting more and more loud the wetter it got. She kicked her legs wildly, exposing her asshole along with her gap. I continued to beat that ass, imagining she really was Ari and I was whooping that ass for her fucking off with P.T. I went into a zone.

"Jahmani! Jahmani! Stop! Aw! Fuck! It hurts, daddy! It hurts! I'll be good! I'll be good!" she screamed, humping into my thigh. "I'm finna cum. I'm finna cum. Aw, shit, daddy!"

Her body got to twitching like crazy. I released her and she fell to the floor, rubbing all in between her legs. I got down and pushed them apart, moved her hand out of the way, and sucked her pussy into my mouth. The whole thing. She humped into my face, cumming harder and harder. I trapped her clitoris and pulled on it with my lips, swallowing her skeeting juices. I had never seen a pussy squirt before. She squirted four times in a row and threw her calves around my shoulders, trapping me.

"Uh! Jahmani. I'm cumming again. Damn, nigga! Leave my pearl alone. I can't handle it. Aw! Shit!"

I sucked harder and slid two fingers into her just enough to stimulate her G-spot. This made her have a sexual seizure.

After cumming for thirty seconds straight, she pushed me away and scooted backward on the carpet. "No more. No more. It's too much."

But I was riled up. I felt like I'd crossed a line, and since I had, it was in me to go all out. I jumped on top of her and ripped her beater from her body. Her breasts spilled out with both nipples standing at attention. I pushed them together and sucked hard.

She closed her eyes and moaned. "Stop, daddy. This ain't right." She wrapped her legs around my body and humped into my piece, wetting it with her gap. She was sticky, and it felt so good.

I fought my way between her legs, jockeying for position. Once there, I reached between us, took my dick, and slid it into her tight box. The fit was snug. I had to slam as hard as I could to bore my way into her womb. Once I broke through, I was fucking that young pussy hard, long-stroking it while the kitty spit its fluid all over my pole. I had her in a little ball, going to work. Our skins slapped together over and over. *Slap. Slap. Slap. Slap. Slap. Slap. Slap.*

"Jahmani! Jahmani! Jahmani! Oh, my fucking. Aw! Yes! Yes! Daddy! My daddy! You're killing me! You're killing me!" She grabbed my waist and dug her nails into me.

I kept seeing images of Ari being folded up the same way by P.T., him fucking her brains out while she screamed his name and said 'fuck me' in her mind. I couldn't believe she could kick me to the curb so easily, that she could leave me behind to fuck with a lame-ass weed dealer. That nigga couldn't have been seeing no real chips, and even if he was, he couldn't fuck wit' my bidness. I loved that girl. If I had to kill P.T. to get her back, then that's just how the cards would fall. I wasn't gon' lose my bitch to no nigga.

Imagined the smirk on P.T.'s face made me so mad I turned savage in Misty's wet pussy. My dick got to going in and out of her at full speed, beating them walls up with no mercy. "Argh!" I growled.

"Holy fuck! Holy fuck! Jahmani! I'm sorry, daddy! I'm sorry! I'll be good! I'll be good!" she hollered and came all over me again. Her face was contorted into a mask of bliss. Sweat glistened on her neck.

I pulled out, picked her up, sat her in the corner of the couch, and put her legs on my shoulders. I held the sides of the couch and really got to killing that monkey. That pussy was fire, wet and oozing. She kissed my lips and bit the bottom one. Her nails dug into my back and scratched me hard. I could feel my blood dripping out of the wound, and I didn't care.

"Misty. Misty. Here I cum, shorty. Here I cum."

I dug as far into her as I could and blasted off, jerking

while my hips rocked back and forth, getting as much of her as I could. She sucked all over my neck and dug her teeth into my jugular.

I kept her in a ball for two more minutes, my dick still hard and throbbing deep within her body. Then I pulled out and sat back on the couch, breathing hard. She laid her head on my thigh and sucked me back into her mouth, removing her juices loudly, moaning deep within her throat.

"Mm. Damn, this a big dick." She grabbed it and kissed the head before sitting up and straddling me, sliding my piece back into her. "Uh. Jahmani. Uh. What about now, daddy? Uh." Her eyes closed and then opened as she bounced up and down.

"What about what?" I asked, gripping that fat ass. Damn, she was so fucking thick. It was crazy. She was just a teenager.

"Me. Me. Do I look better now? Uh. Does my skin matter?" She moaned, rising and falling on me.

I kissed her lips, sucking all over them. "Nall, ma. Fuck that skin. It's good. It's good. This pussy good. Fuck, it's good. Now, ride me faster while I suck these titties.

She threw her head back and got to twerking as hard as she could, bouncing up and down. Her moans kept me hard. Her tight pussy kept me trapped. Her scent kept me captivated. My anger at Ari kept me between her thighs for the rest of the night.

Ghost

Chapter 12

Ari didn't show back up until a week later. When she did, she looked noticeably skinnier. I was sitting in the living room upstairs in Misty's portion of the house. She walked past me and smiled weakly. "What's up, Jahmani?"

I curled my lip at her. "Ari."

"Can we talk for a minute?" she asked, running her fingers through her hair that looked like it needed to be washed. She had bags under her eyes, and her clothes looked a bit wrinkled. Something wasn't right. I could feel it deep within my gut.

"Yeah, let's talk." I got up out of the chair and followed her into the basement with so much anger running through me that I wanted to snap.

We walked past Misty as she opened the door to her bathroom and stepped out dressed in a purple and black Gucci dress that made her look stunning. She had her long, curly hair pulled back into a bushy ponytail. Her makeup was done right. Her toes were matching her fit. She looked good enough to eat again.

"Aw, Ari, when did you get in?"

I waved her off. "It don't matter. Look, me and her finna holler. Don't disturb us, you understand me?" I asked, opening the back door for Ari to step through. She brushed past me and made her way down the stairs.

Misty nodded. "Yeah, I got you. Just don't forget about me." She turned and walked into the living room with her head hung low.

I took a deep breath and closed the door behind me, trying to get her last words off my mind. I didn't know what was going on with my brain. I felt a twinge of something for Misty, and I didn't want to.

When I got downstairs, Ari was pacing back and forth with

her head down. "Look, Jahmani, before you say anything, I just want to let you know I'm sorry. I shouldn't have stormed out of here like that, and I shouldn't have done what I did. But I had to."

I don't know where my tears came from, but I was so mad they fell out of my eyes, and I couldn't stop 'em. "Shorty, this whole time I thought you was a stomp-down bitch, when it turns out you ain't shit. You just like the rest of them Bronx project hos. I wish I would have seen that from the get-go. I would have saved myself a lot of drama."

She popped her head back as if she were offended. "Bitch. That's how you feel?" she scoffed and laughed to herself.

"I don't see shit funny. I'm seconds away from choking you the fuck out. Word is bond."

"You know what, Jahmani? If that'll make you feel better, then do it. I'm not scared of you, and I ain't afraid of death. So, do what you gotta do. I'm right here."

I walked over to her, grabbed her by the throat, and pressed her ass into the wall, squeezing with all my might. I felt like she was trying to flex on me, and since she'd been off fucking with some other nigga, now she thought it was cool to shit on me or something. I pulled my gun out of my waistband and pressed it to her forehead, cocking the hammer with tears running down my face. "Ari, I swear to God, I'll kill you before I let you fuck off with another nigga. I love you so muthafucking much, and I can't handle that shit. You understand me? I don't know what it is about you, but I love you. My heart aching for you."

She gagged, and her eyes were bugged out of her face like to two golf balls. She scratched at my fingers until I let her go and turned my back on her. "You son of a bitch. You just tried to kill me. What's your problem, Jahmani? I told you what I did, I had to do. It was for you and not me."

That was like a slap to the face. "Did you fuck that nigga, Ari? Huh? Did you fuck P.T.'s bitch-ass?" I turned around to face her.

She cried and didn't respond right away. Then, slowly, her head began to move up and down. "Yeah, I did, Jahmani. I had to."

I smacked her so hard I staggered and fell over the table onto my ass. I jumped up. She'd fallen into a push-up position. "You fucked that nigga, Ari? How could you? You a bogus bitch!"

She climbed to her feet and wiped blood from the corner of her mouth, swallowing it. She held up her guards. "You finna have to beat my ass, Jahmani, because I ain't going. Ain't no nigga gon' put his hands on me. So, let's go." She threw up her guards and rushed me with her head down, swinging wildly.

I tucked my gun in my belt and blocked each blow, pushed her as hard as I could. She stumbled and fell to her knees. When she got up, both were bleeding. She put her guards in the air.

"Let's go, Jahmani. Hit me. Stop pushing me around like a punk and hit me."

She rushed me again with open hands, grabbed ahold of my shirt, and ripped it halfway from my body. Then she blazed me in the jaw. It didn't hurt that bad, but she'd caught me slipping, nonetheless, and she had rings on her fingers.

I grabbed her close to me, stuck my leg out, and flipped her over it. She landed on her back, struggling to get up. "Shorty, I'm sorry for hittin' you, but you got your lick back. Freeze this bullshit before I fuck you up like a nigga. I'm real mad right now. Straight-up."

"Nigga, you put a gun to my head. You just put a gun to my head like I was one of those nothin'-ass dudes in the street.

And after I saved your life. Nah, son, you finna have to kill me. Word is bond," she said, sounding like me.

She jumped up and rushed me with one blow after the next. Instead of blocking them, I took them like a man. She hit my jaw, my eye, my chin, and busted my nose, then jumped on me and bit me on the neck. Her teeth broke the skin.

I held her in the air with blood dripping from my nose. "Are you done, shorty? Huh? You still mad?" I asked, just holding her.

She slapped me across the face, and I dropped her ass to the floor, where she wound up on her knees, crying. "I did it for you, Jahmani. I know you'll never be able to leave New York until you get your niece back and find the ones who killed your mother. Well, it turns out P.T. sells loud for Beans and the Dyse Avenue crew. He works for their Bed-Stuy chapter. Jahmani, he told me where your niece is being kept and exactly who killed your mother. I got their addresses and everything."

I felt my heart skip a beat. "What? What did you just say?"

She sniffled and wiped her nose. "You heard me. I know where they're keeping Lonnie. It's a spot out in Brooklyn. P.T. is one of the men in charge of overseeing her." She climbed to her feet and stood in front of me with snot coming out of her nose. "If I can show you where she is, will you forgive me for sleeping with him? Will you still leave New York with me? Please say yes." She wrapped her arms around my body and started to cry harder than before.

I felt like shit. I softened, exhaled loudly, and wrapped my arms around her small body, kissing her forehead. "Yeah, ma. Everybody makes mistakes. I ain't sweating that shit right now. Help me find these niggas, and we'll go from there." I was on the verge of telling her about what had taken place between me and Misty, but I couldn't risk her withholding the information that would help me find Lonnie and my mother's killer. I told myself I would tell her everything after I got Lonnie back. It would be only right that I did.

She stepped out of my embrace and wiped her tears. "In two days, they're going to be moving the little girl to P.T.'s apartment because they've gotten wind the building where she's being held now is going to be getting raided by the police, so P.T. and his cousin Dough Boy are going to responsible for her. I'm told Dough Boy was the one who killed your mother. She tried to fight him when he rushed in and tried to kidnap Lonnie, and he killed her. He killed her and still took that little girl. It's so bogus, Jahmani."

My fists were balled so tight I could hear my knuckles cracking. My eyes were tearing up. I imagined my mother trying to protect Lonnie and some nigga taking her life. I knew I was going to fuck him over. I would torture him before I killed him. I had to. I had to make him suffer before he was sent on his way. I missed my mother so bad.

I wiped my tears and turned my back on Ari. "Yo, shorty, why don't you go ahead and jump in the shower? You smell like that nigga. When you get out, me and you need to talk a little more about all of this."

She gave me a half-smile. "Yeah, I guess you're right. I'll do that." She took some clothes out of the drawer and headed toward the stairs. "Jahmani, I am really sorry about doing what I did, but please know I wouldn't have ever done it if it wasn't for you. And by the way, I know you may not believe me, but I love you, too."

She smiled and continued up the stairs while Misty squeezed past her. She stopped and mugged her until the door closed. "I hope you ain't falling for her charms again, Jahmani. Please tell me you're not." She stuck a tuft of hair behind her ear and walked across the floor toward me.

I pinched the top of my nose and exhaled. "Misty, I don't know what to think. I've always cared about that damn girl, though."

She placed her hand on my arm. "Jahmani, when will you start to care about me? I mean, didn't these last few days mean anything to you at all?" She wrapped her arms around my waist and looked up at me.

Her long hair fell all over her face. It made her look super fine to me. She was the first redbone I had ever felt, and it didn't help matters now that I knew she had some bomb-ass pussy. I kissed her cheek and brushed her hair out of her face. "I care about you, Misty, but you already know Ari is my woman. Can't shit really come from you and I fucking around together. Nothing but a disaster. Nah mean?"

"Nall, I don't. I don't believe that to be true. I felt something this past week, something I've never felt from any man, and I know you felt something, too. Now, did you or not?"

I was silent for a while, just staring into her eyes. "I honor you for holding me down. I needed somebody to be there for me, and you was. I'll never forget that. Huh, let me give you a few bands just on the strength." I broke away from her and grabbed a knot of hundred from under the couch pillow, peeled off two gees, and held it out to her.

She smacked my hand so hard the money went all over the floor. "Nigga, I don't want your fucking money. I want more than that. I want you to care about me just as much as you care about her. Why can't you do that?" Her face was turning red. I could tell she was getting vexed as the seconds passed.

I mugged her and felt like snapping. I didn't like nobody slapping shit out of my hand. I didn't care who they were. "Yo, shorty, I get you're all angry and shit, but don't be knockin' shit out of my hand. I'm trying to look out for you." I knelt to pick my money up.

"You know what, Jahmani? If I thought I could fight good enough, I'd kick your ass right now because you're fucking with my heart, and I don't like it. If you wasn't planning on giving me a piece of you, why would you spend all that time with me? Why would you fuck me like that? Kissing all over me and shit? Huh? Nigga, it's because you felt something for me. You just ain't keeping it real." She said this while pointing in my face.

I laughed and gave her a warning stare. "Shorty, you wilding right now. Now, our li'l week together was good. I enjoyed your company and all that shit, but now I gotta get things on track with Ari. We fucked around behind her back, and I'm already feeling some type of way about that. That shit was trifling."

She gasped. "Trifling? This bitch just fucked around with her ex on your stupid ass and came back with a dirty pussy, and we're trifling? Nigga, you're lamer than I thought. You know what? Fuck you, Jahmani. You want that bitch, you can have her. I hope she fuck you over like she do every nigga she don't deserve. I swear, I thought you were different. Ugh." She rolled her eyes and turned her back on me.

I grabbed her by the hair and pulled her to my face. "Bitch, who you think you talking to like that? Huh? You think I'm one of these fuck-boys out here in New York? Huh, bitch?" I said through clenched teeth.

"Ow! Let me go, Jahmani. I ain't say that. I already know who you are. You're all over the fucking news," she cried, trying to untangle my fingers from her hair.

I released her. "The news? You saw me on there?" I couldn't believe she had this knowledge. It was a definite wake-up call.

She smooth her hair back in order and nodded. "I saw you

on the news the first time two weeks ago, and you've been on it ever since that day. Ari has been on there four times herself." She walked over to me. "All that shit they're charging you with, I thought for sure you were an animal. That you would never let no bitch run over you. But I was wrong."

I turned my face slightly to the side, trying to figure her out. "Shorty, what's your deal? Why you hate Ari so much, huh?" I just had to know. It was nagging at me. I didn't think no cousin should've acted the way she was. She acted more like an enemy than a loved one to Ari.

"She knows what she did. Nobody knows, but she knows what she did to me. I never forget anything. And she was wrong for it."

I stepped forward and placed my hands on her shoulders. "What did she do? Tell me so I can know, ma."

The door opened at the top of the stairs. Misty ran up and kissed my lips, then placed her phone to her ear as if she were talking on it the whole time. She ascended the stairs past Ari and smiled at her before disappearing.

I watched her with a curious look on my face. I wanted desperately to know what Ari had done to her. I could tell whatever it was, it had left a stain on her heart. I needed to get to the bottom of that when the time was right.

Ari came down the stairs smelling like cucumber melon shampoo. She had a pink drying towel around her neck that she was using to continuously dry parts of her hair. "You okay down here, baby?"

I nodded and turned my back to her, folding the money in my hand and sliding it into my pocket. Everything Misty had said was weighing heavily on my mind. I wanted to address it, but at the same time I didn't want to ruffle any of Ari's feathers until after we pulled the move on P.T. and Dough Boy. "You smell good, ma. Am I safe to touch on you now? Did you wash homeboy punk-ass off your skin?" I scoffed and sat on the couch. I couldn't even look at her after knowing she'd fucked off with P.T. I knew it was bogus of me to even be thinking like that, especially after I'd fucked Misty, but it's just how I was feeling. I had that double-standard bullshit running all through me, I can't even lie.

She stepped into the room and pulled open a drawer. She stepped into a pair of Jordache jeans and pulled them all the way up until they conformed to her ass, leaving me with a view of that round apple. Even though I was feeling some type of way, I could not deny how cold her body was. Ari was fucking gorgeous. Just imagining P.T. getting the chance to enjoy her had me feeling sick on the stomach. I couldn't wait to blast his ass.

"So, I guess this is how we're going to communicate from now on? You're going to constantly throw in my face the mistake I made in honor of you? Right?" She shook her head. "Typical."

I got up and got dressed, ignoring her comment. I didn't feel like talking about all that shit. I had murder on my mind. I knew the only thing that would make me feel better was the sight of P.T lying on the pavement with his brains oozing out of his skull and Dough Boy right beside him, just as twisted.

After ten minutes of silence, Ari grabbed her coat off the coat hook and slid her arms into it, zipping it up. I closed the distance between us quickly and stepped into her face. "Where do you think you're finna go?"

She bent over and slid her feet into a pair of Steve Maddens. "It would have been my brother's 25th birthday today. I'm going to go visit his gravesite and say a few prayers. I would have asked you if you wanted to come, but I'm pretty sure you wouldn't. Right?" She knelt to tie the laces on the boots, looking up at me.

The last place I wanted to be was at Mikey's grave, but at the same time I didn't want Ari out of my sights until I got my niece back. I didn't know what she had up her sleeve, or if she did have anything up it at all. I just couldn't afford to have her anywhere else but in front of me. "Yo, I'm rolling out wit' you, shorty. I gotta support you. You're my woman, despite what took place with that nigga. It's all good, I'ma hold you down. Nah mean?" I got fitted and slid my black hoodie on because it was the only thing close to a jacket I had at Misty's crib. I placed my .45 in the small of my back and was ready to go.

Ari stood up and walked over to me, sliding her arms around me. "Jahmani, you don't know how much this means to me. I didn't want to go there alone, and now I don't have to. I couldn't ask Misty. She's been acting funny ever since I got back, like she's mad at me or something. I don't know what's good. But I appreciate your presence. I mean that." She kissed me and rubbed the back of my neck, smelling all good and shit.

"Yeah, ma. Don't mention it. Like I said, its my job to hold you down, so I'ma do that with everything I am."

Even though these were the words I said, all I could think about was avenging my mother's murder and getting Lonnie back. I cared about Ari. I mean, she was deep within my soul, but after Misty's words and the thing with P.T., I was starting to feel weird toward her. I just had a crazy feeling that something wasn't right.

Chapter 13

Ari took the blue-and-black prayer rug and laid it over the dirt of Mikey's grave. She took a second to step out of her Steve Maddens before kneeling. She took a candle out of her pocket and set fire to the wick, then placed a glass covering over the top of it and put it up against his headstone.

I looked both ways. It was ten o'clock at night and slightly windy. The graveyard looked eerie. There were rows and rows of tombstones. Some were huge, while others were barely visible. We appeared to be the only visitors there. I felt real weird standin' over the grave of the person I'd killed. The fact his sister was about to pray for him, and she was my woman, made me feel that much more odd. I was hoping she'd hurry up so we could get out of there. I kept my hand on the handle of my gun.

Ari bent over and placed her forehead on the prayer rug, starting to mumble something under her breath. Then she sat back on her haunches with her eyes closed and opened them slowly. "Hey, Mikey. It's me, your little sister. I just came to wish you a happy birthday up there in Heaven. I didn't want you to think I'd forget. That would never happen." She exhaled loudly and lowered her head. "My life is all screwed up now, but I'm pretty sure you know that. You're my angel, and I believe you've been assigned to watch over me. I'm sorry for failing you. I guess I'm not perfect, no matter how much you used to tell me I was."

She shook her head and tilted it toward the sky that was filled with what looked like a million stars. Off in the distance sat a full moon. It shined as bright as the stars.

The wind picked up, and I started to feel cold. I was ready to go. I was thinking, *Fuck Mikey.* The nigga was a lowlife scumbag who raped females and robbed everybody. The best place for him was the dirt. It was fucked up that it had to be me who put him there, on the strength of Ari, but life goes on.

"Mikey, I miss you so much. There is not one day that goes by where I don't shed tears over you. You were my everything. My protector, my brother, my knight, my shield, my motivator. You were all I had in this world, and now you're gone. I'll never be the same, big bro, but I'm trying. I'm trying to fight forward and remain strong, but it's so hard. We still haven't found your killer, and now Mach is gone. Life has been so crazy lately. Oh, and in case you didn't know, I took a life." She nodded. "Yeah, some old dude was trying to kill my man, and I had to do what I had to. His soul has been haunting me ever since. I ask that you intercede for me. Ask our Father in Heaven for forgiveness on my behalf. Please."

She was silent for about two minutes, her lips moving with no sound coming out of them. I was shaking. My fingers were frozen. I felt like something kept crawling on me, and I was paranoid. I wanted to get up out of that graveyard. I kept getting a bunch of crazy thoughts in my head. What aggravated me was Ari looked as if she was going to be there for a while. I didn't know how much longer I could stand there without telling her to hurry up. Mikey was dead. It was time to move on. I was over it.

Ari waved me over. "Come here, Jahmani. I want you to say a few words to my brother. I need him to know I'm safe, that you have my back now, and you won't allow for anything to happen to me. Please. It'll mean the world to me."

I shook my head. "Yo, I don't talk to the dead. My mother always told me that's against the Bible." I took two steps back from Mikey's grave. Now she was tripping. There was no way I was about to say nothing to dude's bitch-ass. If it was up to me, I would laugh in his face, blast him again, and put him in the same position. I ain't have no love for son. I only cared about his sister, Ari.

Ari placed her hands together in a prayer fashion and held them up to me. "Please, baby. I am begging you. Please, just tell him you have my back, and we can go directly after that. It's been weighing so heavy on my heart."

"Ari, come on, ma. I'm here to stand behind you, to make sure you're good. I didn't say nothing about talking to him and all that shit. It's against my religion to talk to the dead. The Bible says when you speak to the dead, you're not actually talking to the person you think you are, but your words fall upon the ears of a demon, one that works in Satan's kingdom. It's already been too much bad shit happening. I can't afford no more bad luck. I just can't. I'll stand right here until you're done, but it's getting cold. I'm just saying."

She stared at me for a short while without saying a single word, then she smiled. "Then just come down here with me and I'll tell him who you are. You won't have to say a word. How does that sound?"

I was still hesitant. "Man, how much longer we gon' be here after you do that?" I was impatient and ready to bounce. I didn't fuck wit' graveyards. They gave me eerie feelings. I didn't even know where my mother was buried.

"Five minutes afterward, we'll be out of here. Just do this, I'll close in prayer, and we're out of here."

I blew air out of my jaws and knelt. "Come on, shorty, let's get this out of the way. Yo, this the only time I'm ever doing this, so make it good. Word-up."

She smiled and nodded. "Yeah, okay. We'll see about that. Anyway, wrap your arms around me for a second."

I got behind her with my gun in my right hand and wrapped my arms around her. I could feel a tiny rock sticking into my knees, along with a bunch of other stuff. It felt so uncomfortable. I didn't think Mikey's punk-ass deserved none of it, but I was down to do whatever I had to do to stay in Ari's good graces. I had a mission that needed to be carried out, and her role was essential to its completion.

"Jahmani? What are you doing?" she asked, looking back at me with her neck straining.

"What now, Ari? Damn."

"It is very disrespectful to my brother for you to be having your gun all out at his grave. That ain't cool."

I smacked my lips and slid it into the small of my back. "Happy now?" I hugged her to my chest. "Let's get on with it."

She rolled her eyes and closed them, then faced forward. "Well, as you can see, I found a rough-neck. But anyway, Mikey, this is Jahmani, and he's gon' hold me down now. I love him, and I trust him. You can finally rest in peace. There is no more reason for you to worry. Thank you for being the best brother a girl could ever ask for. Thank you for doing the best you could after our parents passed away, but your job is done. I love you, Mikey. Be free." She kissed her hand and blew it to the skies above.

I knew damn well Mikey ain't go in the direction of Heaven because he wasn't nothing but a demon. I guess she didn't see things logically, but I didn't care. I just rolled with the punches. I wanted this to be over.

She held my hands while she said another prayer. Five minutes later we were walking out of there, and I was relieved.

***

Later that night, I was awakened when Misty pinched my thigh. I turned over, opened my eyes, and waited for them to adjust. When they did, Misty stood in front of me with a finger to her lips.

"Shh, Jahmani. I need to talk to you."

I turned over to hear Ari lightly snoring to my right. I wiped my face with my hands and got out of the bed as slowly as I could as to not awake Ari. We wound up upstairs in the hallway with Misty standing in front of me. I was a bit groggy and annoyed. I don't think I could have been sleeping for more than two hours.

"Yo, what's good, Misty? Why you pinching me and shit?"

She swallowed and started to bite on her index fingernail. "I can't stop thinking about you. I don't know what's going on with me, but just knowing you're downstairs in the bed with her is killing me. I've never felt like this before. I swear." She ran her fingers through her silky hair. Her breath smelled like Scope.

I put my finger in her face. "Bitch, I know you ain't wake me up for this shit? You got to be kidding me. Goodnight." I turned to walk away from her.

She grabbed my wrist. "Please don't go back down there, Jahmani. I need you. Damn, why are you doing me like this?" she cried.

I yanked my wrist out of her hand and grabbed her by her nightgown, pushing her through the door and into her room, kicking the door closed. Once in, I slammed her against the wall. "Bitch, you don't give a fuck about me, it's just this dick. You're eighteen, and ain't no nigga ever fucked you like I did. That's all that is," I snapped with her gown balled in my fist. She wasn't wearing panties, so her bald gap was exposed.

She was silent, just staring at me as if she didn't know how to respond. Tears dropped from her eyes. "That's not true. I do care about you, and it ain't got nothing to do with how you fucked me. I mean, yeah, it was good and all that, but not enough to make me develop these types of feelings. Can you please let me go?" she asked, looking into the distance.

"Look, shorty, I'm telling you it ain't smart to love me. I ain't that type of nigga. I ain't got it all. Never have. Now, I'm fucking with your cousin. That's my woman. That's what it is." I released her and grabbed the doorknob to her bedroom.

"She gon' be the death of you. Mark my words, Jahmani. You're too stupid over her, and she's going to be your biggest downfall." She sat on the bed and it squeaked.

I spun around and closed the door back. "You know something I don't know, Misty? Huh?"

She grabbed a pillow and hugged it to her body. "I said what I said. What you do with it is on you."

I flared my nostrils and stepped in front of her. "I see you want me to fuck yo' li'l ass up, don't you? You really think it's sweet, huh?"

She threw the pillow across the bed and crawled on it. Her short gown rose above her waist. I could see her pussy lips from the back. They were peeking under her fluffy ass cheeks. "Goodnight, Jahmani. I'll talk to you in the morning. Close that door on the way out."

She reached for her lamp, preparing to turn it off. I could see a smirk on her face, and it irritated me. I hopped on the bed and grabbed her by her neck, pulled her into the middle of it, and got between her thighs, pulling her gown up around her stomach. "This what the fuck you want, ain't it, Misty? Admit that shit." I pulled my dick out of my boxer hole and ran it up and down her pussy lips. "Beg me for this muthafucka. Beg me for it," I said, sucking on her neck.

"Get off me, Jahmani. Please. Uh! Don't do me like this. Why won't you just care about me like you do her? Fuck." She reached between her thighs and grabbed my pipe, squeezed it, and tried to force it in her hole. "Stop playing. Do me like you did me the other night. Please. Please, Jahmani."

She arched her back and pulled on me harder. The head of

my dick slid an inch into her. Her warmth surrounded me. She was dripping wet already. Her scent rose into the air, right up my nose.

"Bitch, tell me what the fuck you know about Ari. Tell me before I give you any of this dick." I slammed him into her, pumped five quick times, and pulled him out, restin' him wet against her stomach. My piece throbbed and jumped up and down.

She opened her thighs wide and humped into me. "I swear to God, if you don't fuck me, I'ma kill you. I'ma kill you, Jahmani. Give me this dick, daddy. I need it. I need it so fucking bad."

I grabbed her throat and choked her as hard as I could for thirty seconds. When I took my hand away, she started to cough and gag. I took this as my window to slide back into her. I got to fucking her like an animal. I threw her thighs on my shoulder and a pillow over her face. "Bitch, bite that. Bite that while I murder this shit."

My dick slid in and out of her wet box. Her muscles sucked at my pole. Squeezing it. Milking me. I could feel her cream pouring out of her slot. The headboard banged into the wall as I got to jumping up and down in that good pussy. I think it turned me on even more because I knew Ari lay sleeping right downstairs.

"Uh. Uh. Uh. Jahmani. She gon' set you up. She gon' have one of them niggas kill you. She know you. She know you. She know you. Uh. She know you killed Mikey. Aw, fuck. I'm cumming, daddy. I'm cumming already." She smashed the pillow to her face and screamed into it. Her pussy started to quiver all over my tool.

The news was earth-shattering to me. I felt the air leave my lungs, but my hips wouldn't stop moving. In fact, I sped up the pace and really got to wearing her ass out, stroke-for-stroke, beating them guts in.

She wrapped her thick thighs all around me and licked all over my neck, breathing hard into my ear. I slid my hands under her shoulders for leverage and got to figuratively beating those walls loose, plunging as deep as I could go while her cat squirted all over me.

It felt so good that I could no longer hold back. I sucked her hard nipple through her gown and came all in her pussy, jerking while my ass pumped onward until my piece got so sensitive, I had to calm down. I fell on top of her with my face in the crux of her neck.

Whoom!

The door kicked in, and Ari flipped the light switch on. In her hand was my .45.

"Nigga, I knew I couldn't trust you around my fucking cousin. You just like the rest of them trifling-ass niggas!" she screamed and started to pull on the trigger of the gun while she bit on her bottom lip.

Chapter 14

She aimed the gun directly at me and started to pull on the trigger. Her intent was to murder. I could see it in her eyes.

I jumped out of Misty's pussy and dove off the side of the bed, pulling Misty down with me. "Ari! Ari! Chill the fuck out, ma. It ain't what you think."

I peeked over the bed and saw her still trying to get the gun to shoot. Then it dawned on me that she didn't know how to take it off safety. I had to act fast.

I stood up and was about to jump over the bed when the gun went off. *Boom.* A big hole formed in the wall of Misty's room. The scent of gun smoke surrounded the room, along with actual smoke from the gun. Ari held it with two hands and aimed at me.

"Jahmani, if you come any closer, I swear to God I'ma kill you and that snake-ass bitch! I can't believe you!" she screamed.

Boom. Boom. The bullets tore a hole in the floor right by Misty's baby toe. She threw the nightstand on the floor and tried to move it out of the way so she could get under the bed. "That bitch crazy, Jahmani! I told you."

Ari took a step back and lowered her head as if she were about to look under the bed but thought twice about it. She aimed the gun at me again with smoke rising from the barrel. "How could you do this to me, Jahmani? How could you betray me like this? I thought we had something special." Tears dropped from her eyes. She wiped them away and held the gun in shaky hands.

I backed away from the bed with my hands up. I could smell Misty's pussy rising from my pole, feel her spit dried around my lips. The crack of my butt was sweaty from going so hard between her thighs. I was caught red-handed. There was nothing I could say to change the reality of that. "Yo, put the gun down, Ari. I know I fucked up, but this ain't some shit that you kill me over."

She shook her head. "You're just like every other man, Jahmani. You're trifling, just like all of them. You're no fucking different." She raised the gun and pointed it at my face. Tears streamed down her cheeks again.

I clenched my jaw over and over. I was getting angry. Even though she had me at gunpoint, I found it so hard to submit. "Shorty, get that muthafucking gun out of my face. If you gon' blast me, then blast me, but deep down you know you were wrong, too. You fucked your ex, and now you're trying to clap me because I fucked somebody outside of us. You're a hypocrite. That's all you are." I frowned and sucked my teeth, getting more and more heated. I dropped my hands to my side, no longer caring.

"That's what this is about, isn't it, Jahmani? The only reason you fucked her is because of what happened between me and P.T.? I told you, I did that for you. I would have never let that nigga touch me if I didn't need that information from him. I swear, I wouldn't have. So, I sacrificed myself for the greater good of you, and you're fucking her out of malice? If anybody is a hypocrite, it's you. I'm sorry, I can't let you do this to me." She wiped her face and held the gun with two hands again.

"You know what? Bust then, shorty. Kill me. I don't give a fuck. But I ain't about to bow down to you, so if you gon' kill me, let's get this shit over with." I started to walk closer to her.

She backed away. "Jahmani, back up. I swear to God, if you don't, I'm going to shoot you. I'm going to kill you, Jahmani. Please back up," she cried, sniffing snot back into her nose.

I didn't give a fuck no more. "Nah, shorty. Come on. Bust then, if you got the heart. If you don't, I'ma –"

She shook her head in defeat and pulled the trigger. *Click. Click.* She looked at the gun and mugged it, aimed at me, and tried to bust it again, but it was empty. My angels had to be smiling down on me.

I closed the distance and knocked the pistol out of her hand, smacking the shit out of her so hard that she flew to the floor, holding her mouth. She struggled to get to her feet. Once she did, she ran out of the room and down the short hallway.

I caught up to her quickly, tackled her to the floor, and straddled her body. "Bitch, do you know I kilt Mikey? Huh?" I snapped, holding her wrists to the carpet.

She struggled and fought against my hold. "Let me up! Let me up, Jahmani! I need to get the fuck out of here!" she screamed in full tears.

"Answer my question, shorty! Answer me! Did you know about Mikey?"

She pulled one of my hands close to her mouth and bit it as hard as she could, then brought her knee up to my nuts, crunching them. I fell onto my side, holding them and wincing in pain. Ari rushed to her feet and kicked me as hard as she could in the back.

"Nall, I didn't know, but I suspected. Thank you for admitting it!" She kicked me again in the back and ran into the kitchen, grabbed a butcher's knife out of the drawer, and held it up. "I'm finna kill you, Jahmani. You killed my brother. I knew you had something to do with that." She made her way back into the hallway with the knife.

I got to one knee and then stood up. I felt like I was about to throw up. My balls were in my lower abdomen somewhere. I could barely breathe. She'd kicked me so hard it knocked the wind out of me. I held my stomach and limped, taking a step back. "Ari, if you come at me with that knife, I'ma fuck you up. Your brother was foul, shorty. A rapist and a low-life, stick-up kid. That nigga tried to smoke me first. I just did what I had to do."

She shook her head and raised the knife higher. "I'ma kill you, Jahmani. You took my brother away from me and then screwed me over. This was all a sick game to you. All of it. I hate your guts." She ran at me with the knife, screaming as if it were a battle cry. "Aw!"

Bam.

Misty swung a baseball bat into Ari's back, knocking her to her knees. The knife slid out of Ari's hand and across the floor. She fell to her stomach and rolled onto her back, crying with her eyes closed.

"Bitch, you know your brother was a rapist! You helped him rape me. He got what he deserved! I'm glad he's dead." She raised the bat over her head, ready to bring it down.

I stepped in and grabbed it from her, took ahold of her waist, and pushed her behind me. "Yo, she fucked up. You ain't gotta kill her."

Misty peeked from around my body down to Ari. "That bitch is sick. Her and her brother. She knew what he was doing to me when I was little, and she never stepped in to stop him. You thought that shit was cool, but it wasn't. You've hated me ever since I found out about you and Mach."

Ari struggled to get up off the carpet. She held her ribs and exhaled loudly, stopped, and fell back to her knees. She looked like she was in excruciating pain. I felt sorry for her and wanted to help.

"You don't know what you're talking about, Misty. Shut up," she gasped, trying to get back to her feet.

"What the fuck are you talking about, Misty? What about her and Mach? I thought he was her cousin." I mugged Ari.

142

"Yeah, I thought he was our cousin, too, but they didn't act like they were cousins. Tell him, Ari." She stepped from behind me and balled her fists. Her face was red with anger.

Ari made it to her feet and eyed her with hatred. "You always did have a problem with running your mouth, bitch. I swear, if I didn't think he would jump in, I'd kick your ass for old time's sake." She removed her arm from around her midsection and balled her fists as if she were ready for action.

Misty pushed me to the side. "I ain't li'l Misty no more. I ain't gon' let you hold me down while any man takes advantage of me. I'll fight your ass now, and I won't lose. I swear that on my mother. What you wanna do?" She held her arms out like a lowercase T.

I was kind of sick at hearing the Mach news because, if I was understanding Misty correctly, she was saying Mach and Ari had been fucking around and Mikey had been forcing himself on Misty. It did kind of rub me the wrong way when I'd first tried to talk to Ari and Mach rolled up on some jealous shit with him and his crew. He ain't come at me like he was her cousin. He came at me like he was her man. That was odd. "Yo, you was fucking that nigga, ma?"

Ari waved me off. "Get out of the way, Jahmani. Let me and this snake-ass broad handle our bidness. Then me and you can talk. Come on, Misty. You think you can whoop me now? Bitch, then bring it. I'm tired of your li'l, pretty ass, anyway." She put up her guards, then winced in pain. I could tell she was trying her best to fight through the injury the bat had caused.

Misty threw the bat on the floor and nudged me aside. She put her hair in a long ponytail. "For most of my childhood I let you and Mikey take advantage of me. You helped him force my thighs apart, laughed while he took my virginity. I'll never forgive you for that. Bitch, bring it."

Misty rushed her, swinging wildly, her fists balled up so

143

tight that her knuckles were white. Her first punch caught Ari in the nose. The second one caught her cheek, and the third her forehead. The blows knocked Ari backward. She struggled to catch her balance. She fell, and Misty tried to jump on top of her, but Ari held up her knee and flipped Misty over her body and onto her back. She landed with a thud.

Ari jumped up and straddled her before pummeling her with blow after blow. "Punk. Bitch. You. Gon'. Bring. Up. Something. From. When. I. Was. Fourteen?" *Bam. Bam. Bam.*

Misty's head bounced off the carpet. At first, she was fighting back, and then she went limp. I surmised that Ari had knocked her clean out.

"You. Gon'. Fuck. My. Nigga? Don't. You. Know. I. Love. Him. In. Spite. Of. Mikey?" More blows. Now there was blood popping up. She wrapped her hands around Misty's throat and began to choke her with all her might. "I hate you, bitch. I hate you."

Misty lay still, gagging. Slobber came out of her mouth. Blood leaked out of her nose, yet Ari kept right on choking.

I yanked her off Misty and slung her to the carpet. "That's enough. You're killing her!" I yelled, rushing to Misty's side.

Ari rolled across the floor and slid into the wall before jumping to her feet. "You're choosing that bitch over me, Jahmani? After what you did to my brother?" She placed both of her hands on her head and paced back and forth with her eyes bucked wide open.

I pulled Misty into my arms and wiped the blood from her nose. She coughed and shook. I could tell she was breaking up. Her left eye was black, her lip split in the corner on the right side.

"Ari, I'm not gon' let you kill her. She's your little cousin. Damn! What the fuck is wrong with you?" I snapped and picked Misty all the way up, carrying her into the living room and laying her on the couch. Misty burst into tears. "Yo, Misty, you knew you couldn't fuck wit' shorty bidness. This is your fault. You gotta pick your battles, ma." I brushed her hair out of her face.

She reached out for me with her mouth full of blood. "I'm sorry, Jahmani. I swear, I'm so sorry. I'm just tired of being hurt. Tired of her taking advantage of everybody." She laid her face on my hand. Blood leaked onto it.

Ari appeared in the doorway with the butcher's knife in her hand. "You gon' choose her over me, Jahmani? Huh? After all we've been through? You took my brother and all that. I thought you cared about me, Jahmani. Fuck, what's good?"

Misty slid closer to me and placed her face on my chest. "I don't care if she kill me Jahmani. I'm just tired. Let her do what she gotta do. I don't care about nothing no more." She closed her eyes and struggled to breathe. I could hear her nostrils wheezing. I wondered if Ari had broken her nose. It sure sounded like it.

"Misty, shut the fuck up wit' that crazy talk. Ain't nobody about to die up in here. Ari, come sit ya ass down, ma. We need to get an understanding. All of us."

She paced back and forth, shaking her head. "Nall, Jahmani. I thought we were better than this. I can tell you care about that li'l yellow bitch. You care about her more than me. I can't stomach that, man. I just can't. You two can have each other!" She threw the knife on the floor and rushed toward the door.

I bounced off the couch and ran as fast as I could, caught ahold of her arm, and pulled her back to me. "Ari, I love you, shorty. Damn. I keep telling you this. Why the fuck you acting all crazy and shit?" I shook her to get my point across.

She broke into tears. "You fucked her, Jahmani. You fucked her, and you killed my brother. This whole time.

You've been with me this whole time, and you've never been man enough to tell me you're the bastard who killed him. That makes you a pussy." She smacked me across the face.

My cheek burned from the fire of her assault. I tossed her to the carpet out of rage and kicked the door closed. "Bitch, you ain't going nowhere. We finna work this shit out. I told you I love you. I mean that shit. I love you enough to take you off this earth if you think you'll ever be able to leave me. I mean that shit."

She jumped up, slapped me across the face, and swung again. This time I caught her wrist and held it tightly in my grasp.

"Ari, don't slap me no more. I can only take so much. If you slap me again, I'ma stomp ya ass into the carpet. That's on my mother." I slammed her against the wall and took a deep breath. "Look, I'm sorry about Mikey. I'm not sorry I killed him, I'm sorry I wasn't man enough to tell you I did. But your brother was foul, ma. You already know he was. Son tried to take me out, and like I said before, it was either him or me."

Ari shook her head. "He was my brother, Jahmani. He was all I had. I know he wasn't the best person in the world, but he was my brother. You didn't have to take him away from me, Jahmani. I swear, I really love you. I love you with all of my heart." She fell to her knees and broke down crying her little heart out, sobbing loudly.

This made me feel like shit. I sank down and wrapped my arms around her, turned her so she faced me, and hugged her more firmly. "Damn, baby. I'm sorry. I'm sorry for killing him. I swear, if I had a choice, it would have never happened. I never wanted to hurt you. I fucked up with Misty, too. I just kept on imagining all types of bullshit when you ran out of here. I felt that you were with some other nigga. I did what I did with her. I fucked up. Please forgive me," I pleaded, holding her as tight as I could without crushing her.

Misty came into the front room with pants and a tank top on. "I'm not about to let her take you away from me, Jahmani. I swear to God, I'll kill her first. This bitch don't deserve a man like you. I'll love you ten times more than she ever could. She only fuck with niggas that's related to her."

Ari tensed against me and struggled to get up, but I held her firm in my grasp. "Ooh! I'm so tired of this bitch. You want me to forgive you, Jahmani? Let me kill this bitch! You let me kill her and we can start from scratch," she promised, shaking.

I shook my head. "Nall, that's enough fighting for one day. Y'all gotta chill that shit. We gotta figure this impossible situation out. It's the only way."

Misty knelt beside me and ran her hand over my naked back. "I'm not giving you up without a fight. She gon' have to whoop my ass every single day. I'm crazy about you, Jahmani."

Ari snapped. "Crazy bitch, you don't even know him. You see, that's always been your problem. You always fall so hard for a man you barely know. That ain't how love works. It's why you always wind up hurt and alone. Damn, you're dumb."

Misty's response was to lay her face on my back. I could feel her breathing in and out. It was labored. "I don't care what you're talking about, Ari. I ain't going nowhere. You won't be around long. I'm sure of that." She got up and staggered toward the back of the house.

Ari pushed me away and turned her back on me. "That was the wrong bitch to fuck, Jahmani. That girl is like a leech. You will never get her off you. You'll see." She shook her head and lowered it, placed her hand on her waist, and paced back and forth.

I slowly got up and looked her over. I didn't know what to

say or do. I was looking at her different after finding out all the new information from Misty. The whole thing with Mach was throwing me for a loop, and how Misty had described the scenario of Ari helping Mikey take advantage of her. It was like I was seeing her through new eyes, but at the same time, the love I felt for her hadn't gone anywhere.

"You know what, Jahmani? I'm still going to hold up my end of things. I told you I was going to help you get Lonnie back and avenge your mother's death by bringing her killer to street justice, and I am. My word is bond, as you New Yorkers say. After you do what you gotta do, I think it'll be in your best interest for us to part ways. You go yours, and I'll go mines. When I look at you now, all I see, and feel is betrayal. You're scum. And for some reason, I still love you," she scoffed and walked off toward the basement.

I stood there with my head hung low, my hand resting against the wall. I was wishing my mother was still alive. I needed to be in the presence of somebody who truly loved me. I was confused. Broken. Angry. I didn't know which way to go or what to do.

I looked to my right and saw Misty appear in the doorway. My head was still hung low. I couldn't think straight. I felt sick on my stomach. I didn't want to lose Ari. As tough as I may have seemed, I still had a heart, and that heart revolved around my newfound love for her. I took a deep breath.

Misty stumbled in and rubbed my back. "I heard what she said, Jahmani, and I just want you to know I'm here for you. I truly care about you. Your past doesn't matter to me. In my head, you killed Mikey for me. You have no idea how much him being alive hurt me." She hugged my waist. I could smell the scent of her perfume mixed with sweat. She took my right arm and wrapped it around her body, the palm resting on her shapely hip.

"Misty, yo, I love Ari. I don't know why I love her so much, but I love her, shorty. If she walk out on me, it's gon' crush me. It's crazy because I ain't even known her a year, but it's like I been a part of her since my birth. I don't know what to do."

Ari walked past us without saying a word. She opened the front door. "Look, I'm about to go and make sure everything is still good. I'ma hit you first thing in the morning, and you'll come take care of this business. I gotta keep my word, but after that, I don't wanna see you no more." She looked from me down to Misty. "I hope that bitch make you happy."

I broke out of Misty's embrace and rushed to Ari. "Yo, before you leave, we need to talk, ma. Just give me five minutes of your time. I can't have you hit them bricks feeling like you're feeling. It's gon' cause you to make some stupid mistakes."

"Nah, it's good, Jahmani. I'm mentally good. Now that I know who killed my brother, I can think straight. I'ma handle this for you, and then I'ma repent and leave New York. Ain't nothing here for me. I'll be in touch." She snatched away from me and slammed the door.

I fell to my knees, feeling like a dagger had been stabbed through my heart. Misty came and knelt beside me. "You're letting the Devil break you down, Jahmani. You need to be careful."

Ghost

Chapter 15

Two days went by, and I didn't hear nothing from Ari. I was starting to worry something had happened to her or she'd said fuck me altogether. Both scenarios had me sick as a dog.

I took to sitting in the basement and tooting lines of cocaine to ease the pain. Misty had been to Urgent Care, and they'd prescribed her Percocet. She'd given me a couple of them, which I took and crushed into a powdery form, tooting them just as hard as I did the cocaine. I was fucked up, and even through the foggy drug haze, I couldn't stop thinking about her, worrying and imagining the worst-case scenario.

On the afternoon of the second day, after giving me my distance, Misty came into the basement with a bag of food from NY Gyro Xpress. "Yo, Jahmani. I know you trying to stay down here in your cave and all of that, but I just had to bring you somethin' to eat. Plus, I miss yo' crazy ass. I need to sniff you up a li'l bit."

She put the bag of food on the table and sat next to me on the couch, crossing her thick thighs. She opened the bag and pulled out a wrapped gyro. It smelled so good that my stomach got to growling like crazy. I was happy to see her, but I didn't want to let her know that.

"Shorty, I told you, I'm trying to collect my thoughts. I ain't want you fucking wit' me. What's good?" I put a mug on my face.

"Yeah, well, nigga, you gon' have to kick my ass, because I'm feeding you, li'l daddy. I need you to have all your strength whenever this bitch call you for this mission. Did I tell you I got a bad feeling about this whole thing? Huh?" She opened the wrapping on the gyro, exposing how meaty it was. She'd decorated it with plenty of cheese and cucumber sauce.

I was salivating. Starving. I wiped my nose and sat back

on my stubborn shit.

She picked the sandwich up and scooted closer to me. "Huh, open up, Daddy. I need you to eat half of this, and then I'll leave you alone. You got my word on that."

She brought it to my lips. Its aroma drifted up my nose. "Yo, shorty, once I eat this shit, you gotta go. You understand that?" I opened my mouth and took a nice bite, gathered a lot of meat, and chewed with my eyes closed. That boy was fire.

She wiped my mouth with her thumb and sucked it into her mouth, took a bite of the sandwich, and chewed, smiling at me. "It's good, ain't it?" She pressed it to my lips again, straddling me.

I took another bite and chewed, holding her ass. She had me feeling some type of way. I didn't understand why her li'l ass cared about me so much so fast. It was blowing my mind, and I had to find out what was good. I waited until I swallowed. "Yo, let me take a sip of that soda pop, shorty. What kind is it?" I ran my tongue across my teeth. The gyro's flavor was all over my taste buds.

She grabbed the drink and held the straw to my lips. "It's Cherry Pepsi, daddy. The one and only. It go perfect with this gyro and these chili cheese fries." She pulled the fries out of the bag and sat them on the sofa next to us.

I finished my sip and swallowed. "Misty, I got a question, and I want you to answer it with the truth. Don't beat around the bush, and don't lie to me. Okay?" I moved her curly hair out of her face and looked into her eyes.

She nodded, took a sip of the Pepsi, and put it back on the table. "I haven't lied to you since I met you, Jahmani. I won't start now. What's on your mind?"

"Yo, I need to know if the only reason you care about me is because you know I got feelings for Ari? Is your whole mission to fuck wit' me, just so you can fuck her over?"

152

She jerked her head back and frowned. "Baby, hell nall. What type of female would that make me?" She climbed off my lap and wiped her hands on a napkin.

"Ma, I ain't trying to get you all angry and shit. I'm just asking a question." I didn't feel like arguing wit' her. I could tell she was heated because her face was red.

She blew air out of her nostrils and paced back and forth. There was a slight limp to her walk. "The truth is, I don't know why I care about you so much. I mean, when I first saw you, the first thing I noticed was how fine you were. I knew you were mixed with something right away. Then I liked how your muscles were all over the place. But after the lust at first sight, I got to looking at you past your exterior. I saw how much you cared about Ari and how you treated her like a queen even though I knew she was fucking around on you with P.T. That got me angry. I feel like she's always the one to stumble upon a gold mine. I felt jealous." She placed her hands on the small of her back. "Jahmani, I ain't never been snatched up the way you snatch me up. I ain't never been talked to by no man the way you talk to me. You pointed out my flaws before you took the time to point out my beauty. You looked through me instead of at me, and for me that was huge because I'm so used to men only seeing my looks. They think just because I look a certain way, my brain doesn't work or that's all there is to me, whereas you attacked my strengths, and that made me weak for you. I like you, Jahmani, because you're different. You're a goon. I need that in my life. I know Ari could never care about you or love you as much as I could, especially since you murdered her brother."

"That's another thing. Who told y'all that?" I scooted to the edge of the couch and drank from the Pepsi. I had a piece of gyro meat stuck in my teeth. It was irritating me.

"Apparently some chick you know by the name of

Samantha told Beans that, and he put the word out that it was you who killed Mikey and robbed some dude named Chase. The Dyse Avenue boys have been looking for you ever since. Ari has known for a week now. It's amazing she hasn't told you. That's why I don't trust her. Never have, never will." She came over and sat beside me on the couch. "Jahmani, do you ever think you'll be able to have any feelings for me? I mean, I know I'm only eighteen, but you can mold me into being a rider for you. I don't want to have to leave your side. I'll be whatever you want me to be, long as you protect me and give me the game." She kissed my cheek and straddled my lap.

I grabbed that ass and held it in my hands. Samantha's face came into my mind. I hated that bitch. I knew if I ever ran across her again, I would do her a lot of harm. She was a dirty female, shysty as they came. Ever since I'd been a part of her life, I'd went out of my way to make sure her and my niece, Lonnie, were taken care of, and all Samantha had ever been was a thorn in my side. She was one of the reasons I'd been forced to kill Mikey. All of it started and took place at the Bronx River Houses, inside of her apartment.

"Yo, Misty, you got a lot of learning to do, shorty. I mean, I can see that one hunnit shit in you, but rocking wit' me, knowing what I'm up against, it's going to be a task. I could die at any moment. Long as you're rolling with me, you're going to constantly be under the gun. I got enemies on all three sides. Bloods, Crips, and the police. Ain't nowhere safe. Knowing all of that, you're sure you wanna still ride wit' the god?" I rubbed her soft cheek with my thumb.

"Let me be the Bonnie to your Clyde. Where you go, I'll go. I ain't scared of those streets. All we gotta do is leave New York in the dust. We've made it here, now we just gotta make it out. We make it out, we can make it anywhere else. But let me prove myself to you. Let me show you I can be ten times

154

the woman she ever could." She leaned forward and kissed my lips, licked them, and moaned with her nose up against mine.

"Yo, you talk a good game, shorty. I'ma see what it do. Right now, I need that feminine crutch, nah mean? If you swearing on your word that you gon' hold me down, then we gon' start out as friends. Ari still weighing heavy in my system. Let her work her way out of it, and then me and you can do our thing. Let me taste that pussy, though."

I placed my fingers on the waistband of her shorts and pulled them down, revealing her bald sex lips. I sniffed the crack of them, made her put her foot on the cushion, and sucked her box into my mouth. It was hot and tasted like body wash mixed with pussy.

She moaned and placed her hand on top of my waves, forcing my face into her crease, riding it slowly. "Okay, daddy. We can start off slow. It's good. Uh! Daddy, it's good." She threw her head back. Her eyes rolled into the back of her head. "Uh!"

I pulled her ass cheeks apart with my fingers and licked all around her clitoris. She stuffed my face so far into her box that I couldn't breathe, and I didn't care. Her scent was strong and addicting. My tongue went into overdrive on her clit.

"I'm about to cum, daddy. I'm about to cum!" she hollered and bucked into my mouth, fucking my face like a savage.

Her cum ran out of my mouth and down my neck. It slid along my collarbone, dripping onto my chest. I yanked my shorts down. My dick sprung up in the air. "Ride this dick, momma. Come on. Show daddy how much you want him."

She straddled me, reached under herself, and slowly eased down until she engulfed my whole piece. She moaned. Her eyes rolled into the back of her head. "I love this dick, daddy. It's so big." She cocked her back and started to bounce up and down on me while sex sounds came from between our legs.

It felt like she was gripping me with her fist. It felt so good that I got to groaning in sync with her. "Misty. Uh. Misty. Baby, this pussy. This pussy. So. So good." I grabbed her hips and made her ride me faster and faster. She bounced higher and higher. Her pussy made slurping sounds as it devoured my pole.

I stood up and laid her back on the sofa, pressed her knees to her chest, and got to killing that pussy, stabbing in and out of it. It got wetter and wetter. Her juices oozed out of her and wet my undercarriage. The couch slammed into the wall while she whimpered underneath me.

"Jahmani! Jahmani! Oh. Oh. Daddy! Daddy! You're killing me again! You're killing me again! Fuck!" She turned her face to the side and screamed into the body of the sofa.

I kept on hitting it harder and harder. It seemed like the deeper I plunged, the wetter she got. Her walls felt like silk. The muscles were thick, strong. They sucked me into her body and then tried to push me out as I withdrew. She had that snapper. "Misty. Misty. I'm finna cum, li'l boo. I'm finna cum, ma. Uh, fuck, baby." I slammed into her five hard times and started to cum in gobs inside of her.

"Uh! Daddy. Daddy. I feel it. I feel it. Fuck, it feel so good."

Her cat started to suck even harder on me. It vibrated and then got so wet I almost slipped out. She hugged me tighter and shook like crazy. I sucked her neck and bit into her with my teeth, sucking on her earlobe.

"You say you gon' ride wit' me, right?" I continued to slide in and out of her in slow motion.

"Yeah, daddy. I'm riding wit' you until the end. Just teach me. Show me the way. I'm following you, Jahmani, I swear."

Those words sent chills down my spine because I believed them. I don't know why I did, but I did.

I bent her over the couch and fucked her from the back real slow while I played with her asshole. I wanted to get inside of that big ol' thang, and I knew I would one of these days. It was inevitable.

After we finished our session, we climbed into Misty's big bed, and she slid into my arms, wrapping hers around my neck while she lay her head on my chest. "I'ma ride for you, Jahmani. You'll see. I know you think I'm just jacking or blowing smoke, but you'll see. I've been a rider all my life. I just never had the right man to ride for." She slid her thick thigh over my body and licked my nipple.

"We gon' see, shorty. My life is crazy. If you're going to be a part of it, it's about to be a short, but wild ride. I'm letting you know now that your life expectancy is about to go all the way down. You might not live to see nineteen, shorty. You sure you wanna roll wit' me?" I squeezed her big booty. Her warm pussy rested on my hip, its scent intoxicating.

"It's already written when my time is going to be up. Long as I'm beside you, then it is what it is. I'll die happy." She looked up at me and smiled. "I'm yours, Jahmani. Let's get it."

I held her a little tighter and couldn't deny the fact she had me feeling some type of way. Still, I was missing Ari.

Ghost

Chapter 16

Ari hit me up ten days after she'd left Misty's crib. It was five o'clock in the morning and storming like crazy outside. Misty had been the one to hand me the phone. She stood on the side of the bed wit' her hand on her hip as if she didn't want me talking to her. I frowned, then ignored her ass.

"Yo, what's good, Ari? Where you been at?" I rubbed the cold out of my eyes and yawned. I was feeling extremely tired this morning, and all my injuries were killing me. I needed a few of those Percocet in my life. I would hit Misty's ass up for a few after I hung the phone up.

"It's time, Jahmani. I got everything set up the way it needs to be. Dough Boy and P.T is holding Lonnie in a duplex over in Harlem. I'm texting you the address right now. I want you to meet me there. I'll let you in through the back door when the coast is clear. You need to get in, handle your business, and get back out, though. They're going to be expecting a delivery from Beans. He's supposed to show up with a bunch of his goons sometime today, but I don't know when."

Misty grabbed the phone and clicked it onto speaker. She frowned at me and mugged my iPhone 8. She shook her head and mouthed the words *I don't trust this bitch.*

"Yo, ma, why are they moving her out of the Bronx? Whose idea is this? And have you seen her?" I asked, rising out of the bed and sliding my legs into my jeans. I needed to feel Ari just a little bit more. There was no telling how she was feeling after finding out I had been the one who killed her brother and I was fucking Misty. They said hell hath no fury like a woman scorned. I wondered if Ari was scorned. I wondered if she had some vindictive shit up her sleeve. I wondered what her angle was.

"Yeah, I've seen her. I gave her breakfast this morning and

a bath last night, per P.T.'s wishes. She's still beautiful. Lost a few pounds from the last time I'd seen her, but appears healthy, nonetheless. And I think it was Beans' idea to move her out to Harlem. They are up to something in the Bronx, and he's feeling like the spot they were once in will become a target by both enemies and the police."

"Yeah, a'ight. What time are you talking, shorty?" Something didn't feel right. I felt like there was more at play than what she was letting on. I paced back and forth in front of the phone that sat on the dresser, trying to collect my thoughts.

"Four. Four should be good because we're supposed to leave here around two-thirty. I'll do my part when it comes to his mind. Keep him discombobulated. Dough Boy is another story, though. That fool is a head case, and him and I don't get along. I think he's on the down-low because he appears to hate all women. Before you get at P.T., you're going to have to take care of him. Trust me on this." She paused. "We're on the first floor, so when I let you in through the back door, you'll go right in through the kitchen, and they'll be set up right there at the table in the dining room, whipping Beans' heroin."

"Bitch, what's in it for you? You ain't finna do all this shit for nothing. What the fuck is your thirsty-ass getting out of all of this?" Misty snapped before I rushed to her and placed my hand over her mouth.

Ari was quiet, and then I could hear her exhale loudly into the phone. "Really, Jahmani? You got her listening to our calls now? That's how you're getting down on me?"

I grabbed Misty by the back of the neck and threw her out of the room and into the hallway. "Bitch, stay yo' ass out here until I'm done since you can't keep your mouth closed," I snapped, ready to spank her ass until she screamed for me to stop. I was that heated by her outburst.

"But, daddy, I was just –" she began.

I slammed the door in her face and had to calm myself down.

"Jahmani! Jahmani! Did you hear what I said?" Ari hollered into the phone. "Hell-o?"

I picked it up. "Nall, I ain't hear what you said. What's good?"

"In exchange for me doing this stuff for you, I want her ass."

"What do you mean by that?" I inquired, needing to make sure.

"What I mean is I wanna beat her to death. She's too far into our business, probably jumping your bones every chance she gets, and on top of that, my back ain't been the same ever since she hit me with that baseball bat. That's the deal: you get Lonnie, and I get to do whatever I want to do to Misty. Deal or no deal?"

***

Four hours later, Misty pulled her Jeep Grand Cherokee up a block away from where we were set to meet with Ari. She threw the Jeep in park and looked over to me. "I can't believe we're about to trust this bitch, Jahmani. Do you realize this could be a set-up in which we both lose our lives? I mean, she hates me, and you killed her brother. Why would she go all out of her way to help you get your niece back? This just doesn't make sense. Can't you see that?" She placed her hand on my thigh.

I cocked both of my Glocks and put them back on my waist. I had nothing but murder flowing through my mind. I kept seeing the image of my mother's slain body in my head, then the smirk on P.T.'s face when I went to the door, trying to get Ari back. I wanted to blow his head off just on the strength of him fucking my woman. I was on some sucker shit, and I couldn't even deny it. "Look, Misty, what you're saying makes sense, but at the same time, I gotta handle my business. These muthafuckas killed my mother and had my niece for almost two months. It's only a matter of time before they kill her, too. I mean, I still don't know why they've kept her alive this long."

"That's what I'm saying, you don't even know if she is alive. For all you know, she could be already dead, and you could be walking into a trap. I could lose you, and all for what? I say we get the fuck outta here, leave New York tonight, and just drive until we're far away from here. I got some people in North Carolina, people Ari don't know about. We can go there, and you can start over, baby. Please, listen to me. Ari is going to be the death of you." She grabbed my wrist and kissed the back of my hand, rubbing her face into the palm of it. "Please."

I sat there for a moment, thinking everything over that she'd said. Would it be smart to turn the Jeep around and drive away from avenging my mother's murder? Should I leave my niece to fend for herself, essentially leaving her to die? What about Linx? Should I forgo that beef, let him walk away scot-free? Could I turn my back on my past and start somewhere fresh? Was it smart to leave the city of New York behind and enter North Carolina blindly beside Misty? How much did I really care about her? And was the life of Lonnie a fair exchange for Misty's? Could I stand to trust Ari to hold up her side of things?

"Baby, please say something to me. You've been quiet for ten minutes," Misty said, placing her hand on the side of my face.

My phone vibrated with a text from Ari. *It's time.* Those were the only words that came across my screen.

I took a deep breath and slid my phone back into my

pocket. "I gotta handle my bidness and let the cards fall where they may, so let's go," I ordered, feeling my heart pounding in my chest.

Misty blinked and tears rolled down her cheeks. "I got a feeling we're making a mistake. But, like I said, you lead, and I'll follow. So, let's do this."

She put the Jeep in drive and pulled it into the alley that led to the duplex I was set to meet Ari in.

To Be Continued...
A Bronx Tale 3
Coming Soon

Submission Guideline

Submit the first three chapters of your completed manuscript to ldpsubmissions@gmail.com, subject line: Your book's title. The manuscript must be in a .doc file and sent as an attachment. Document should be in Times New Roman, double spaced and in size 12 font. Also, provide your synopsis and full contact information. If sending multiple submissions, they must each be in a separate email.

Have a story but no way to send it electronically? You can still submit to LDP/Ca$h Presents. Send in the first three chapters, written or typed, of your completed manuscript to:

LDP: Submissions Dept
Po Box 870494
Mesquite, Tx 75187

DO NOT send original manuscript. Must be a duplicate.

Provide your synopsis and a cover letter containing your full contact information.

Thanks for considering LDP and Ca$h Presents.

A Bronx Tale 2

BOW DOWN TO MY GANGSTA

By **Ca$h**

TORN BETWEEN TWO

By **Coffee**

BLOOD STAINS OF A SHOTTA **III**

By **Jamaica**

STEADY MOBBIN **III**

By **Marcellus Allen**

BLOOD OF A BOSS **V**

By **Askari**

LOYAL TO THE GAME **IV**

LIFE OF SIN II

By **T.J. & Jelissa**

A DOPEBOY'S PRAYER **II**

By **Eddie "Wolf" Lee**

IF LOVING YOU IS WRONG… **III**

LOVE ME EVEN WHEN IT HURTS **II**

By **Jelissa**

TRUE SAVAGE **VI**

By **Chris Green**

BLAST FOR ME **III**

A BRONX TALE III

DUFFLE BAG CARTEL

By **Ghost**

ADDICTIED TO THE DRAMA **III**

Ghost

By **Jamila Mathis**
LIPSTICK KILLAH **III**
WHAT BAD BITCHES DO **III**
KILL ZONE **II**
By **Aryanna**
THE COST OF LOYALTY **II**
By **Kweli**
SHE FELL IN LOVE WITH A REAL ONE **II**
By **Tamara Butler**
LOVE SHOULDN'T HURT **III**
RENEGADE BOYS **III**
By **Meesha**
CORRUPTED BY A GANGSTA **IV**
By **Destiny Skai**
A GANGSTER'S CODE **III**
By **J-Blunt**
KING OF NEW YORK III
By **T.J. Edwards**
GORILLAS IN THE BAY II
De'Kari
THE STREETS ARE CALLING II
Duquie Wilson
KINGPIN KILLAZ III
Hood Rich
STEADY MOBBIN' **III**
Marcellus Allen
SINS OF A HUSTLA II

166

A Bronx Tale 2

ASAD
HER MAN, MINE'S TOO **II**
CASH MONEY HOES
Nicole Goosby
TRIGGADALE II
Elijah R. Freeman

Ghost

By **TJ & Jelissa**

BLOODY COMMAS I & II

SKI MASK CARTEL I II & III

KING OF NEW YORK I II

By **T.J. Edwards**

IF LOVING HIM IS WRONG…I & II

LOVE ME EVEN WHEN IT HURTS

By **Jelissa**

WHEN THE STREETS CLAP BACK I & II III

By **Jibril Williams**

A DISTINGUISHED THUG STOLE MY HEART I II & III

LOVE SHOULDN'T HURT I II

RENEGADE BOYS I & II

By **Meesha**

A GANGSTER'S CODE I & II

By J-Blunt

PUSH IT TO THE LIMIT

By **Bre' Hayes**

BLOOD OF A BOSS **I, II, III & IV**

By **Askari**

THE STREETS BLEED MURDER **I, II & III**

THE HEART OF A GANGSTA I II& III

By **Jerry Jackson**

CUM FOR ME

CUM FOR ME 2

CUM FOR ME 3

CUM FOR ME 4

A Bronx Tale 2

An **LDP Erotica Collaboration**

BRIDE OF A HUSTLA **I II & II**

THE FETTI GIRLS **I, II& III**

CORRUPTED BY A GANGSTA I, II & III

By **Destiny Skai**

WHEN A GOOD GIRL GOES BAD

By **Adrienne**

A GANGSTER'S REVENGE **I II III & IV**

THE BOSS MAN'S DAUGHTERS

THE BOSS MAN'S DAUGHTERS II

THE BOSSMAN'S DAUGHTERS III

THE BOSSMAN'S DAUGHTERS IV

THE BOSS MAN'S DAUGHTERS **V**

A SAVAGE LOVE **I & II**

BAE BELONGS TO ME

A HUSTLER'S DECEIT I, II

WHAT BAD BITCHES DO I, II

By **Aryanna**

A KINGPIN'S AMBITON

A KINGPIN'S AMBITION **II**

I MURDER FOR THE DOUGH

By **Ambitious**

TRUE SAVAGE

TRUE SAVAGE II

TRUE SAVAGE **III**

TRUE SAVAGE **IV**

TRUE SAVAGE **V**

169

Ghost

By **Chris Green**

A DOPEBOY'S PRAYER

By **Eddie "Wolf" Lee**

THE KING CARTEL **I, II & III**

By **Frank Gresham**

THESE NIGGAS AIN'T LOYAL **I, II & III**

By **Nikki Tee**

GANGSTA SHYT **I II &III**

By **CATO**

THE ULTIMATE BETRAYAL

By **Phoenix**

BOSS'N UP **I , II & III**

By **Royal Nicole**

I LOVE YOU TO DEATH

By Destiny J

I RIDE FOR MY HITTA

I STILL RIDE FOR MY HITTA

By **Misty Holt**

LOVE & CHASIN' PAPER

By **Qay Crockett**

TO DIE IN VAIN

SINS OF A HUSTLA

By **ASAD**

BROOKLYN HUSTLAZ

By **Boogsy Morina**

BROOKLYN ON LOCK I & II

By **Sonovia**

170

GANGSTA CITY

By **Teddy Duke**

A DRUG KING AND HIS DIAMOND I & II III

A DOPEMAN'S RICHES

HER MAN, MINE'S TOO

By Nicole Goosby

TRAPHOUSE KING **I II & III**

KINGPIN KILLAZ

By **Hood Rich**

LIPSTICK KILLAH **I, II**

CRIME OF PASSION I & II

By **Mimi**

STEADY MOBBN' **I, II**

By **Marcellus Allen**

WHO SHOT YA **I, II**

Renta

GORILLAZ IN THE BAY

DE'KARI

TRIGGADALE

Elijah R. Freeman

GOD BLESS THE TRAPPERS I, II, III

THESE SCANDALOUS STREETS I, II, III

FEAR MY GANGSTA I, II, III

THESE STREETS DON'T LOVE NOBODY I, II

Tranay Adams

THE STREETS ARE CALLING

Duquie Wilson

BOOKS BY LDP'S CEO, CA$H

TRUST IN NO MAN

TRUST IN NO MAN 2

TRUST IN NO MAN 3

BONDED BY BLOOD

SHORTY GOT A THUG

THUGS CRY

THUGS CRY 2

THUGS CRY 3

TRUST NO BITCH

TRUST NO BITCH 2

TRUST NO BITCH 3

TIL MY CASKET DROPS

RESTRAINING ORDER

RESTRAINING ORDER 2

IN LOVE WITH A CONVICT

Coming Soon

BONDED BY BLOOD 2

BOW DOWN TO MY GANGSTA

A Bronx Tale 2

www.ingramcontent.com/pod-product-compliance
Lightning Source LLC
Chambersburg PA
CBHW070033260626
47159CB00005B/2030